ENDLESS IN AUGUST

ENDLESS IN AUGUST

TAYLOR KICKBUSH

NEW DEGREE PRESS

ENDLESS IN AUGUST

ISBN

978-1-64137-994-6   *Paperback*

978-1-64137-885-7   *Kindle Ebook*

978-1-64137-886-4   *Digital Ebook*

CONTENTS

———

A NOTE FROM
THE AUTHOR

———

I wanted to be a journalist for two-thirds of my life, yet I had no intention of ever writing a book. The thought of drafting much more than two thousand words caused such severe anxiety that I'd break out in a cold sweat. I'd create any excuse I could to successfully navigate a story to a shorter end. After all, I didn't (and still don't) think people like to read much more than they have to.

If you're into the new-age, woo-woo, "believer of the universe" sort of stuff, then you'll understand me when I say the universe made me write it. If you're not, then my apologies. I'm still pointing a finger at whatever (or whoever) is overseeing this sphere. While I'm at it, I think I'll give them a huge air hug for bringing me to this juncture—along with all of the friends and family who dealt with my sleep deprivation, hair loss, and stomach pains while I wrote this book.

The inspiration for *Endless in August* derived from a culmination of things, including a man I picked up in a bar, a spontaneous birthday trip, a kayaking adventure, and a car accident. After all of these events, in that order, I found myself asking one question:

The uncertainty of life and what happens next is frightening, isn't it?

I never did become a working journalist, but I still like to ask a lot of questions. For me, this one in particular seemed to be the most important one of all. That's in part why this book exists. I've spent much of my life pursuing answers to my questions because of fear. Fear of discovering the truth. Fear of diminishing time. Fear of the final deadline. When asked if death terrifies me, even after all of my years going to church and being aware of the end, I admittedly didn't have any clue how I felt about it. That was, until I was hurtling down a thruway on August 4, 2019, and could have easily been killed by a car that rear-ended me and pushed me over an embankment. I was carried to a hospital from the scene via ambulance and spent a few hours there rocking back and forth in shock. From that instant onward, I was certain I was not ready to die.

Tell me, what if you knew today that you'd be saying *au revoir* to this world? Would you take any chance you could to expand your life further? Are we in such fear of death that we'd do anything to delay its final countdown?

Just before the car accident, I was floating with my significant other (the man I met in a bar) in a kayak on the Potomac River in Shepherdstown, West Virginia, as part of a quick getaway from my nonstop life in Washington, DC. The setting sun drew a swath of orange across the sky; music from a nearby wedding echoed in the valley. A fisherman cast a line from his motorboat in the distance. For the first time in a long time, I felt at peace. I scanned the water surrounding me, enjoying its soothing lap against the boat's sides just below my elbows. Then I noticed what looked like bug carcasses surrounding the kayak. One by one the lifeless husks drifted by in the sluggish current. My gaze traveled across the river and saw a seemingly infinite number of them.

"What the *hell* are those?" I gawked at my significant other in horror.

He began explaining the lifecycle of this tiny creature with their floating brown husks littered across the water. What I supposed was a graveyard was actually a rebirth. I was in the presence of nymphs molting their exoskeletons as they emerged from their underwater phase. Next, they'd transform into flying, mating creatures called *imagos*—what we commonly refer to as mayflies. How freeing this all sounded!

We continued bobbing alongside an emerged mayfly resting on a small twig as it flapped its wings dry. I admired its grit when it felt ready enough to leap to the sky, kick its fluttering into high gear, and zoom away. My eyes tracked the mayfly's flight until it became a blur in the tree line. My partner watched it disappear, too, and explained what it would experience in the next twenty-four to forty-eight hours of its short lifetime.

Love and death.

"Whoa, whoa, *whoa*." I halted the conversation. "You mean to tell me that the mayfly will die *tomorrow*? Why? Does it know how short its life will be?"

How unfair. The thought of something receiving its wings (literally) and then having its life stripped in a day filled me with anger and a curious sense of compassion.

"Is there a way to make the mayfly live longer?" I asked.

He retorted with a litany of scientific concerns regarding how genetically expanding a life so impactful to the environment might not be a good idea. I disagreed at first, though. If you could give anyone—or in this case, anything—a longer chance at life, wouldn't you?

I've experienced both beautiful and heartbreaking comings and goings, indisputable love, and death that caused unimaginable pain. So have you. I imagine these are emotions we'll continue to swallow so long as the universe and stars align just so. At times, though, we may choke while trying to understand the *why* of it all. I've racked my brain trying to figure it out. And, just as any post-journalism graduate would do in a period of uncertainty, I started to ask questions, seek answers, and write.

Endless in August was composed as an outcry of my questions about mortality at a time when I felt most uncertain. As I journeyed through each chapter of *Endless in August*, I unraveled and rewrote my understandings of life and loss in a tale that ushered a laugh into my throat at times and tears onto my keyboard at others. I intend to share with you, through the story of Benjamin and Gracie, the vulnerable, delicate, and beautiful existences we live in a moment, a lifetime, or an eternity.

I don't know if you should fear death. I can't predict the hours you have left to live, nor what it would feel like for you to be in love. I can only imagine what you should think when you see snow for the first time, or how you would dance in the desert under the stars. What I can tell you is I trust there are answers to your grander questions; sometimes you just have to cast a line before you receive what you went fishing for.

To those who helped me find Grace.

I told Gracie to step aside while I prepped my stance for a cast with one foot set back on the bank and the other in the water. After making sure my little girl wasn't within hooking distance, I set the line about two feet and lightly grabbed the cork grip—my thumb in file with the rig. I snapped the rod backward to gain tension. It arced behind me, as if achieving enough momentum to whip the setting sun. Then I paused.

Pausing. Is. Essential.

1

TRAVELING TO SPACE

———

"There it is, Daddy!" she squealed, spotting her muddled reflection rippling in the blackened river water.

I took a drag from my cigarette, held it in my lungs, then slowly released my breath. Smoke trailed from my cracked lips as I sat in an unfolded blue camp chair. Observing Gracie at such an innocent age made me wonder if I was ever that fragile and naïve to the world.

Her pink chiffon tutu bobbled with the wind as she squatted on the edge of the riverbank. Mud had crusted like clay over her knees, and her bangs hadn't been trimmed in so long, they fringed over her cornflower-blue eyes. She didn't seem to mind, though.

Gracie stood up from admiring her reflection and giddily stumbled alongside the water in her black, size-four rain boots. Her white velvet leotard had a yellowish grass stain on the front from crawling on the ground all day while chasing uncooperative dragonflies and holding crickets hostage. Soon she'd want to capture fireflies and keep those as pets too.

Gracie took a break from her waterside adventure, whirled her small body around, and smiled at me. She had picked a daisy. She held it to her nose gently, as if it might fall apart if she sniffed it too hard or held it too tight. She ran to me with a rosy-cheeked, gap-toothed smile. Two of the daisy's petals flew off in the wind before she reached me.

"This is yours," she insisted bashfully. Gracie held it up by the limp stem, as if it were an offering fit for the gods.

"Very pretty, honey," I said, coughing up some of the tar living in my chest. It's about time my lungs revolted. I began smoking the summer after finishing high school, just a week before joining the Army. My then neighbor and best friend, Finny, slipped a Camel between my fingers at my going-away party in my parent's backyard.

"This'll get you through some tough times," he assured me twenty-six years ago in the light of a fire that was bigger than the two of us combined. I hadn't stopped since. Maybe I was still wading through the tough times.

I took the daisy from Gracie and stuck it in the netted cupholder of my chair next to my Camels. She twirled away, her blonde hair whipping behind her as she ran back to play in her own little world.

As I watched her pet cattails and mutter to her imaginary friend Jack, I wondered what she talked about. She had a mind unknown to wars, starvation, picketing, and politics. What the hell else was there?

"Sweetie, c'mhere a minute," I ordered not too sternly. She ran to me, her tutu almost a blur in the late afternoon gold.

"Yes, Dad?" she asked, out of breath.

"What are you and Jack talking about tonight?" I made sure to nod toward where I thought Jack would be.

"It's a *secret*, Dad"—she glanced beside her—"but . . . I don't think he'll mind if I tell you."

She put her hands on the arm of the camp chair, stood on her tiptoes, and leaned in to whisper loudly in my ear.

"We're talking about the stars, Dad, and how wonderful it would be to fly into space and touch one. I promised Jack one day we'd meet an astronaut and that the astronaut would let me touch a star and maybe even bring one home! Wouldn't that be great? I think it'd be so cool to see how beautiful the world is from up above the stars."

She lowered herself to her heels and took a step back from my seat, awaiting approval.

I thought carefully before replying, stroking my short, umber beard.

"Oh, I see. Well, that's nice, sweetie. You and Jack go play a little longer."

She giggled, took the imaginary boy's hand, and skipped back to the flower-covered bank of the Elk River.

The mind of a six-year-old was, by far, more charming and restless than my own. I wasn't going to be the one to tell her she probably wouldn't travel to space, no matter how much she wanted to. I wouldn't have to. They'd teach her all about the impossibility of her dreams in grade school, crushing her simple wish to own a piece of the sky.

Gracie cupped the air to hold the hand of a boy I never would see and continued to harvest more wildflowers. Meanwhile, I wished I could become an astronaut overnight so I could bottle a constellation for my daughter.

That's the problem with this goddamn world, anyway—it's hard enough to breathe, let alone touch the stars.

2

SEEMED LIKE A
GOOD IDEA

"Fuck, there she goes again," I sputtered under my breath. Gracie stood by the river with her face jutted toward the sky. Her eyes were tightly squeezed shut, her smiling mouth agape, and her tongue stuck out so far, I thought she could've been a relative of Gene Simmons. In her grip just inches from her drooling chops was her soon-to-be victim; a five-inch earthworm tried desperately to wriggle from impending death to Gracie's innards.

She peeped one eye open to see if I was witnessing the fiasco.

I snickered, hoisted myself from the camp chair, and limped the twelve feet to the Elk waterside. I rested my palm on Gracie's shoulder just as the worm slipped into her mouth. I shuddered.

"Baby girl, what did I tell ya about eating the critters meant for our fish? How are we going to catch any trout without the bait?"

Gracie grinned and puffed her cheeks out at me, then spat the worm onto the grass.

Sighing, I picked the mush up and flung it to the shallows. Some minnow would be grateful for it.

"Jacky Jack told me to do that, Dad!" She thumbed to Jack's spot to her right. "We're both hungry!"

"Well, Jack must think like a trout, then! Since you've gobbled the last of our worm can, go catch some critters while your dad casts a fly for dinner."

Gracie let out a prompt squeal. She always loved watching me fly fish.

I let her burst away with Jack to pretend to look for more worms under stones and nearby bushes while I fumbled for my car keys in the chest pocket of my button-down.

Ah, there they are, next to a couple Nicorettes.

"Be right back, Gracie!" I hollered as she lifted a flat piece of shale upriver to inspect another squirming specimen. I winced my tired, midnight-blue eyes in disgust.

Our Outback was parked in the uphill lot in front of Sutton Dam. It would be a brief, ten-minute walk there and back.

Gracie'll be fine alone for that amount of time.

I hobbled through the overgrown grass of the hill with my aluminum cane, resting every other minute to suck in some air. Two extra minutes were spent lunging over the passenger-side handle of our apple-colored Subaru, Red. She'd been holding up since 2002. She'd been a good girl to us over the years, transporting us through the everyday bustle of life, plus taking Gracie and me on our annual August fishing trip several years in a row now.

I circled to the back of Red and unlatched the trunk. What a fuckin' mess it was back there with our camping gear and sleeping bags. I had to comb through three backpacks and one lunch pail before remembering I had shoved my fly wallet in one of the side doors for easy access.

Slipping the segments of my rod from Red's trunk, I closed the hatch and found my gray, nylon trifold fly wallet on the driver's side. It was a baptism gift from my grandmother, Eleanor, who'd died before I formed the brain cells to remember people and things. It was the only prized item I had, besides Gracie. Eleanor had hand-stitched "Benjamin" on the front of it in thread the color of a fire engine. I always wished it said "Ben" instead, but I liked it, nonetheless.

I slammed the door and shoved some disheveled russet curls back beneath my worn, hunter-green fishing cap. I located a soggy cigarette in my jean pocket and made my way slowly back down toward Gracie with cane and gear in tow.

"Okay, sweetie, let's fly. 'Member how?" I yelled.

Gracie zoomed to me without answering my question. I knew she remembered how it all worked. I was pretty sure it was the only thing I taught her besides the word "shit," and that was by accident on her fourth birthday when I knocked over a can of root beer onto my favorite burgundy flannel.

I tossed her the trifold fly wallet and she popped the button up, flipping it open to single out her favorite fly. It was a beadhead wrapped with peacock feathers and a tail dyed fluorescent pink. The wings of the head were a stark white—excellent for catching us a meal in mid-August.

After I pieced my fly rod together, she playfully dangled the buggy within reach, letting me snatch it from her on the first attempt.

"Okay, Daddy, I think next we, um, we put the fly in the water?" Gracie asked.

"Ah, close, sugar. First we gotta double-check the rod and make sure everything is lookin' intact."

My cane fell to the grass when I unleashed my grip to inspect the fly rod. It gleamed in the sun as I swung it up and held it to the sky to examine the backing and line. I jiggled the rig a bit, making sure nothing was misaligned.

"Okay, I think we're set. Whaddya think?"

She stepped beneath the rig and gazed upward, closing one eye and cocking her head as if inspecting a diamond.

"I think it looks pretty. I think the fish will like it," she nodded confidently.

I chuckled. I had a feeling she was going to grow up valuing beauty over most things. I hoped that wasn't the case, but she sure liked things just right.

"Let's fly, baby girl," I exclaimed as I swung the fly rod over my shoulder and placed my hand between Gracie's shoulder blades to shuffle us closer to the Elk. I didn't bother struggling to put my waders on. The trout were visibly nibbling at the nymphs scattered across the surface.

I told Gracie to step aside while I prepped my stance for a cast with one foot set back on the bank and the other in the water. After making sure my little girl wasn't within hooking distance, I set the line about two feet and lightly grabbed the cork grip—my thumb in file with the rig. I snapped the rod backward to gain tension. It arced behind me, as if achieving enough momentum to whip the setting sun. Then I paused.

Pausing. Is. Essential.

I sucked in a grit-toothed breath to hold while I let the line unfurl in the air behind me. For three seconds, things were still. Gracie's bright blue eyes. The swooping barn swallows. The smoke trailing from my Camel. The teenager paddling an orange Sun Dolphin a mile away.

The line reached its end in a slight jolt. I quickly extended my arm forward in a smooth motion, kind of like throwing a baseball, but different. The line snapped forward and soared, landing thirty-five feet out. Gracie whooped and awed at the distance.

Not bad for doing this one week a year.

"Whoa, you rock!" is what I think Gracie shouted when I swiveled to accept her high-five with my left hand. Damn, she was getting old.

"Let's play the quiet game so we can catch somethin'," I laughed.

Ten minutes of baiting and tugging passed with no bite on our line, despite the ripples of hungry fish surfacing for dinner.

The sun's last shred of gold neared the mountain. My stomach grumbled loud enough to scare away the cricket resting on my forearm. The thought of having to drive to the nearest gas station to grab us some Pringles and Fiber One bars for a meal irritated me enough to flush my unshaven cheeks. Thankfully, I felt a soft tug on the line not long before I sold myself to some salt and vinegar chips.

"I think we got one!" I hollered.

Gracie's eyes darted toward me and the line tugged again, this time much harder. I set the tiny hook carefully, then reeled the trout toward me slowly, making sure to give him time to tire out. He jerked back and forth below the water. I eased the line out a bit to give the fish some hope, then challenged him once again, flicking the pole skyward. The fish put so much strain on the rod that it had the arch of a lowercase *n*. I stepped back, twirling the reel handle so quickly that Gracie would only be able to see the peach whirl of my finger.

Splashing ensued.

The trout was so close I could discern its scent as it splish-splashed in the shallows. I lurched forward and seized its slippery body, unhooked its pout, then hurled the gleaming creature to shore.

A decent nine-incher will have to be good enough for us tonight.

I unhooked the fly from the fish's lip and let him squirm to enjoy the last of his time. When his energy slowed, Gracie kissed his heaving gills.

I limped away from the bank to gather kindle for our fire, glancing back every so often to watch my daughter as she caressed the trout. She shed tears over its now motionless figure, letting droplets fall from her chin and onto its fins. Surprisingly, this was all silent, and I knew she was trying to impress me in remaining so despite her sorrow for the fish's plight.

I let her pay her solemn respects and then gutted the trout out of sight to avoid more trauma for the evening. I wanted Gracie to grow up to be strong. That'd take epiphanies she'd have to learn without me.

We cooked our dinner over the fire in silence and let the campfire aroma caress our nostrils. The fish charred a bit on a skinny oak stick I'd found. Fireflies slowly emerged from the darkness, blinking like the flashing plane lights in the night sky above us.

Gracie didn't notice any of this. Her eyes were locked on the fish.

I savored a breath to study this young, somber human in front of me. Firelight flickered on her fair, shoulder-length hair that I still hadn't learned to braid. The orange glow illuminated her skin, tanned from spending summer days in the sun. Shadows danced under her eyes and on the freckled bridge of her nose. They made her appear much, much older. Like her mother. My stomach twisted at the thought of Naomi.

Gracie peered up at me from the fish. "Dad, why can't we do this forever?"

I took one of those ever-important pauses to deliberate my answer.

"Because Mama would miss you, baby girl. But guess what, we can do this every August as long as you live. Just you, me, and Jack. How does that sound?"

She grinned, satisfied with the idea. She didn't have to say what we were both thinking. I too would rather hide away on the river until the day I died. Unfortunately, tomorrow we'd have to deal with her mother.

3

WHEN WE WERE YOUNG.

———

My eyes resisted opening, like my eyelashes were metal fixings rusted shut. I groaned and pried them free to find an eruption of tangerine light permeating Red's frosty windows.

Goddamn it, we're gonna be late.

I jolted from the laid-back driver's seat and spun to find Gracie resting her head on a back-seat window, conked out. She managed to squeeze in beside a white pail and burrow into her lavender sleeping bag last night.

I sucked in half a breath to admire my girl before having to cope with the awakening process. Her fine baby hairs poked out every which way, her chin shone with drool, and her eyes danced in a dream beneath her lids—probably to *Barbie in the Nutcracker.* I saw a lot less of Naomi in her face now and a lot more of me.

I bet I drooled like that, too.

I laughed at myself before a sense of urgency bubbled in my gut. The sun inched further above the mountain. I tugged on Gracie's cotton cocoon.

"Sweetie, we gotta head for the hills in a bit, and I know you want to say goodbye to the Elk. We're already running very late," I mumbled while massaging a chunk of tar in my throat.

And I need my medicine so I can breathe.

A moan and a slight rustle.

"Suit yourself, I'm driving home then," I declared matter-of-factly, rotating back to the windshield and leaning in to extract Red's keys from the coin-filled cupholder.

"Haddy, I haf to fee," is what I caught between an exaggerated yawn and a few airy words.

Well shit.

I halted mid-reach.

"I thought I told you to pee before sleep time, Grace," I said firmly, placing my hand on the steering wheel. Fog blanketed the Elk below.

She noisily rummaged for a few sheets of toilet paper in the pocket in front of her. "I *did* pee before sleep time. I have to go *now*, too," she said, cracking the door and dashing to the closest tree. I contemplated scaring her while she did her business, but last year I did that, and she cried about a ginormous, hairy sasquatch haunting her dreams for months. It was funny at the time, anyway.

Gracie rejoined me quicker than normal and bopped into her back-seat haven but left the door open.

"We gotta wait a minute for Jack, Dad. He's going to the bathroom, too."

I looked at her in the rearview mirror and gave a nod, then returned my attention to the Elk, where a trout burst into the air above the dark water. Its silver belly gleamed like an aluminum wind chime struck by sunlight. The fish arched back into the water. I tried to take a deep breath and imagined how nice it'd be to permanently live in some cabin in this part of West Virginia. The car door slammed.

"'Kay, we're ready!" Gracie exclaimed, wrapping her arms around her petite body—hugging Jack, I supposed— and slipping back into her sleeping bag.

Beholding Gracie's eyes and telling her that we'd be leaving was something I did annually. Yet every year the words pulled deeper from a sunken cavern in my throat, making them that much more difficult to say. I always promised Gracie that the trees and fireflies would become more beautiful in 358 days when she returned. It was the Band-Aid I typically used to relieve the pain of this particular goodbye. It usually worked, though guilt lingered in me each year when we made the trek to find the trees and fireflies no more spectacular than the time they were before.

"Okay, onward we go then," I sighed, awaiting the hurt.

Gracie made no fuss at all. Instead, she blew kisses to all of the trees and waved goodbye to the Elk as we pulled out of the gravel drive. Then she snuggled further into her cocoon. I was amazed, proud, and curiously hurt by the lack of tears as I pondered the change for a good chunk of the one-hour drive to Clarksburg. The day before, she didn't seem ready to go home.

My mulling and Gracie's sleep were both interrupted by my careless and sudden encounter with a pothole in the Clarksburg CVS Pharmacy parking lot. Gracie bonked her head against the window, and I winced for her. "Sorry, darlin'. I gotta . . . run in to . . . see Ms. Mia. C'mon with me, like usual, 'kay?" I wheezed between painful breaths as I parked Red. With help from my smoking habit, my lungs weren't cooperating like they used to.

We scuffed to the door of the store just as the pharmacist was unlocking the building.

"On time this Sunday, I see," she commented, opening the door for us with a bright smile.

Ms. Mia was pretty new in town and right out of some private college in New York. She'd decided to pursue a degree in pharmacy later than some, but I found her absolutely brilliant. She shared with me a few months ago over coffee that she was celebrating her thirty-fourth birthday this year and insisted Gracie and I attend a barbecue in her backyard. We'd missed her famous birthday chicken skewers just a few days ago while we were away fishing.

"Ah yes, you know, I have to be prompt," I blurted anxiously. "Oh and, I uh . . . am sorry we . . . missed your birthday. We were out on . . . the Elk River for our . . . annual father-daughter trip. We really woulda come otherwise."

Ms. Mia led us through the vitamin aisle back to the pharmacy and began filling a bottle with pills.

"Meh, it's okay about my party." She shrugged. "A few friends popped in, and then I watched *Seinfeld* reruns. It could've been worse."

I wondered if she saw *Seinfeld* with anyone in particular, and then realized the pill bottle was resting on the blue laminate counter. I passed her a damp ten-dollar bill and she cha-chinged the register.

"You know, you wouldn't have to rush here at 8:00 a.m. every Sunday if you extended your prescription amount with your doctor," she said, leaning over to ogle at Gracie holding my hand below the counter.

"Ah, right, well . . . it's okay. It's a nice excuse . . . to get outta . . . the house together, right, honey?" I bumped Gracie with my hip.

"Mm-hmm, we like Sundays, Ms. Mia," she chimed.

I thanked Ms. Mia for her punctuality as usual, murmured something nervously about hoping to grab coffee soon, scooped up the pill bottle, and ushered Gracie as quickly as

I could toward the car. If we didn't hurry, there'd be consequences. My lungs were already cinder blocks.

Once outside the CVS, I unlocked Red from a distance and told Gracie to run ahead and get in because I'd left my cane behind. She did so without hesitation, and upon her door closing, I stood in the middle of the parking lot, unscrewed the pill bottle, and popped a penny-sized green tablet in my mouth. I closed my eyes and swallowed through the chalky thing, letting the morning sunshine seep red through my lids.

My mind drifted to a state of fret, despite the soothing glow and the concrete being rapidly excavated from my airway.

What am I going to tell Gracie if Naomi leaves us again?

4

THE FRAGMENTS OF US

———

I hadn't had much experience with women, but in forty-four years, I had only met one who made an explosive sunset dull in comparison. If you were driving in bottleneck traffic in Times Square, you'd still notice her weaving through the masses, so much so that the rest of the trove of shoppers would become a blur. It was impossible to ignore the ingredients concocting such a woman: a chestnut mane curling effortlessly down to her petite lower back, a soft nose with fairy-kissed freckles, a cupid's bow she preferred to paint crimson red, numbing evergreen eyes, and skin brushed by the olive soaking in grandpa's dry gin martini. Naomi was the type of woman that could transform any bumbling mortal man into Don Quixote. She had become my windmill.

Naomi burst into my store, Marmo's, for what I thought was the first time thirteen years ago. Days before Labor Day, I was passing the hours plying the family glassmaking trade in lieu of cookouts and camping trips. I specialized in handblown player's marbles and glassware. I was certain on that morning, as I admired a customer I would later come to know as Naomi Bianchi, that she was a woman not there for either.

The weekend aroma of fresh-cut grass and barbecue outside the shop couldn't mask her sweet dandelion perfume. It smelled familiar, and I could imagine a stream of liquid gold spritzing onto her neck. My heart rate increased at the lucid thought. Thankfully, the afternoon sun beat through the front window and the shop's glass wares ejected gleams of turquoise, red, and white fractals around us. The shimmers distracted her from the dumb dropped jaw and ogling eyes that were all I currently had to offer. She tried to peer at me through the hundreds of round blue and red handblown ornaments that hung from the ceiling, though they obstructed our view of one another. I could've mistaken the woman for one of Picasso's cubist faces, and I was suddenly taken with modern art.

She dodged through the ornaments, leaving them clanging against one another, and walked briskly to me. One of my creations cracked against another and detonated on the floor. I was unfazed by the chaos. Her eyes unraveled me instead. A single tear glided over her red lips and made its way to her chin. A speck of teal light from a nearby vase made it gleam.

"I'd like to ask you for some help, Ben," she said to me. The tear committed to its fall onto the pine countertop, splattering on my pinky.

I raised my eyebrows at my name. Not many strangers called me by my first name.

"Uh, how can I help?" I rubbed the teardrop into the short sleeve of my white cotton T-shirt and leaned forward.

She dipped a hand into the glass bowl of ninety-nine-cent, clear marbles by the register, cupping maybe seven.

"Well—for starters, can I bum a cigarette?" She cast one marble back in the bowl and wiped her cheek with the wrist of her free hand. I fiddled in a cargo pocket of my old khaki Army fatigues, removed a cigarette and my 7Eleven lighter, and handed them to her. She stuck them in the back pocket of her Levi's.

"Thank you so much," she murmured as she flung marbles two and three into the bowl with the others. "I was hoping you might also have a pen and a piece of paper?"

"Ah . . . yes, I think I have both," I agreed with some uncertainty. I disappeared beneath the register for a minute and reappeared with a chewed pencil and a legal pad that I must've shoved in the lower cupboard years ago. Naomi cast away the remaining four marbles, lifted the materials from the counter, and hunched over the paper in her arms. The pencil scribbled quickly on the paper.

She etched for several minutes, glancing at me every other. She spun the pad around before the quiet devoured my patience.

What the—

I was staring back at a younger me on paper. I almost didn't recognize myself with the clean-shaven jaw, but I knew this was a sketch of me from a photo my Ma took when I first enlisted in the Army when I was eighteen.

How the hell?

"You looked much younger then, huh?" she asked, flashing a pensive smile at the dog tags half visible beneath my shirt. "I've missed you a lot."

Missed me?

I shook my head in confusion at her declaration. "I'm sorry, do I know you?" I asked. My voice stuttered.

She let out an exasperated, almost angry breath. "Oh, Ben . . ." she breathed, and put both palms to her forehead as she planted her elbows on the pine countertop. "I've been looking forward to this moment for so long." She let out a soft sob and her shoulders trembled.

Who the hell is this woman? How does she know me? Why is she crying?

Thoughts darted to the foreground and back, but none prevented me from rushing around the corner to hold this mysterious and beautiful stranger. She was crying, after all.

"It's okay, don't cry, we can . . . talk about it," I stammered, resting a hand supportively on her lower back.

"That's the thing," she sniffled, "I've been waiting to talk to you for months. I've been waiting just to see you for what feels like a lifetime. They said you wouldn't remember me, and I—I just didn't believe them."

The woman straightened, stepped away from me, and moved jerkily toward the bay window. My dark blue eyes fixated on the back of her head as she stared into the street.

Who said I wouldn't remember you?

She advanced toward me with her hand extended moments later. Her long, slim fingers trembled.

"I'm Naomi. Naomi Bianchi, since you don't remember me at all. And—I promised myself I wouldn't come off too strong, but I'm your fiancée, Benjamin."

My wonder quickly transformed into more confusion. I opened my mouth as if I were going to say something, but no words were forthcoming. I was certain my eyebrows were doing all of the talking.

"Huh—too strong?" she asked, more teardrops cupping her eyes. She dabbed them away before they could fall. "I was actually the first person you ever dated, and fun fact, the only person you've made love with—or so you've assured me." Naomi looked up toward the ceiling as if that'd help jail the tears in her sockets. "You still don't remember?" she asked to the heavens.

I hoped my silence scorched her questions.

"This isn't funny," I responded eventually, thinking back to the day of my accident in Iraq. I cleared my throat—almost feeling the grit of sand stinging my face. I put a hand on the back of my head and felt the scar from the gash where bomb shards had embedded themselves in my head. "Why are you here?" I asked Naomi.

"This is the first time I've seen you since you've been home. You hit your head, Ben. I recognize you know that, but I don't think you understand what that has meant to your memory or to us. The doctors warned me not to visit you until you were, what they called, 'healed.' I figured if you had returned to work, then you were feeling better."

This stranger, Naomi, wasn't wrong about the accident. My unit had been under siege by the enemy. An explosive was launched and detonated. I barely lived. My hands and teeth clenched as I remembered the loss of good friends that day.

"That's enough," I commanded, not wanting to believe I would or could ever forget a woman I had loved. "Tell me the truth about why you've come here."

Naomi blinked at me in surprise and slowly reached into her front pocket. She unfolded something and handed it to me. I smoothed out the cardstock and stared at the photo of me that Naomi had sketched earlier. Ma's cursive handwriting inked the back: "My Hero."

"Is this for real?" I asked her, stunned as I stared at my image and proof that it had belonged to my mother.

"Yes, Ben, this is for real. I wasn't allowed to be with you in the hospital when you came home. The doctors said it could be . . . risky to your recovery progress." Naomi crossed her arms. "They told me you'd be permanently caned and that you wouldn't remember who I was. They recommended someone else take care of you until you were ready to meet me again. So, Mia offered to pick you up and look out for you."

That's why Ms. Mia and I started getting coffee together.

"Why should I believe all of this? That you're really my fiancée?"

Naomi scanned Marmo's, obviously choking back tears. She shrugged at me and pulled the cigarette I'd given her. She flicked the lighter and lit it; smoke twirled around a fuchsia ornament hanging just over her head. "It's just the truth. I don't know what else to say," she whispered.

I stared at her in silence.

"So, I don't remember you, or anything that happened before the accident, really. Just limited pieces of my childhood here and there. I remember Ma and Pa. And my house down the road. I can recall, vividly, what happened the day I hit my head. But everything else—"

"Everything else disappeared. Especially us," she finished.

I jerked my head up and down, as if I understood. The sound of Naomi sucking smoke into her lungs sounded almost familiar.

I don't know what the fuck is going on here.

The entire fabric of my being was unraveling in a space where I normally felt invulnerable. Naomi took another drag.

"I want you in my life if this isn't all bullshit," I said to her, "but I'm not sure what progress I'll make in remembering you. Promise me, for your own sake, you'll leave if you feel like I've become a stranger to you too."

The cigarette glowed as she took another huff, then exhaled. She nodded and held out her hand to seal the bargain with a handshake. That was the binding contract I made with my fiancée, Naomi Bianchi, on the first day I recall meeting her fourteen years ago—a woman I'd known my entire life and couldn't seem to remember at all.

Naomi loved the former me with some hell of a burning fire, but the me I had become without her was something she resented. She couldn't bear the thought of losing the giddy first twenty years we loved one another. And, while I had good days of remembering tidbits of us, especially once we had Gracie together, I had many, many more bad ones, where her existence seemed to present itself like an unopened gift.

Sometimes Naomi stayed. Other times she held up her end of the bargain.

5

SCABBED OVER WITH YELLOW PAINT

———

My eyes flickered to the CVS sign disappearing in the rearview. The red *S* disappeared first, then the *V*, then *C*. Once it vanished, I lifted my ass up from the seat, grabbed the yellow pill bottle from a back pocket, and planted it into the cupholder. The spare change shuffled to make room.

"So, sweetie, Mama wants to have something special for your birthday today, ya know," I verbalized as sweetly as I could muster.

In truth, I hated that Naomi decided that we "weren't together anymore," but still wanted to share a home for Gracie's benefit. It just didn't seem right to mislead her with a false love story.

"Yeah, I know, Daddy," Gracie mumbled with disappointment dabbing her words. "Wish you would stay."

Wish you would stay.

The words made my chest clench. Time on the dashboard glowed green, about half-past eight. I was really cutting Gracie's drop-off close.

"Ah, girly, ya know I want to come, but I just stole you from your Mama for a week. Y'all need some girl time."

As much fun as it sounded to munch on cold cheese pizza and listen to first graders tromp through the house, I had to unpack the car and fire some work down at Marmo's anyway.

Pulling into our gravel driveway made Gracie and I bounce with the suspension. The clock displayed our early 8:53 arrival. Anxiety loosened its clamp on my throat. Being just a few minutes ahead of schedule would scab over at least one argument about my timeliness today. I never imagined I'd volunteer to participate in any relationship that required roll call. I smirked at the notion of standing at attention to Naomi.

What a difference just seconds can make on a ticking time bomb.

"There's Mama!" Gracie squealed.

Naomi opened the screen door, wandered outside, and rested her elbows on the wooden porch railing. She wore a black tank top with the skinny straps I liked and light-colored, high-waisted jeans. Her hair was pulled back tightly in a ballerina bun. Her feet were bare. I'd come to consider this particular ensemble her painting outfit. It made it hard to imagine that I could forget such a sight, or more so, be mad at it time and time again.

"Whatcha painting, Mama?" Gracie questioned, cranking down the window.

"What's that, sweetie?" Naomi asked, cupping her ear.

Gracie put her hands to the sides of her mouth. "Jack wants to know what you're painting!"

Naomi stood up from the railing and turned toward the door. "Let me show ya both. Come inside." She grabbed the metal handle, swung the door open, and peered back at us to ensure we'd follow. For a split second, I thought I caught a wink. Intentional or not, I cemented in my brain as best I could the way her eyelashes fluttered.

Gracie sprung open the car door before I could even kill the ignition. "I'm coming!" she announced to the world. I twisted the key to bring Red's engine to a halt and hung back to weigh the pros and cons of cleaning the car out while Gracie raced inside.

Eh, what's another day of being a mess?

I reached for my cane, left Red, and made my way falteringly up the white steps of our two-story house. I slipped inside the door and made my way to Naomi's sunroom, but was halted in the kitchen by the presence of a large, round, Barbie-themed cake on the shelf.

I thought we'd agreed to have a fishing-themed party this year, but I had orders not to be there to celebrate, so what was the point in arguing?

The wooden spiral steps in the living room led upstairs to Naomi in her favorite room with Gracie. Gracie sat in front of an easel with a paintbrush, stroking lemon-colored acrylic paint onto a small, square canvas. Naomi stood hunched below one of the skylights, as if she were offering her work to the morning sun. This work, like many she'd done, was a graphite line drawing of two lovers. I figured Gracie still didn't understand the art, so she decided to make her own.

Naomi's hair appeared red in the tinge of orange light bursting into the space. I unglued my eyes to enjoy, at least briefly, my wife's territory: the twenty-some sketches plastered to the wall, the layers of paint crusted on the glass hand-me-down desk, the smell of murky brush water and old color. My wandering eyes met hers. Instantly I remembered her middle name. It was Joy.

The scratchy sound of Gracie pressing her paintbrush too hard on the canvas interrupted our unintended soul-searching. Naomi placed the lovers on the glass desk beside her and hastened to Gracie's side. Bending down, she said, "Why don't we go cut your cake, baby girl? It's almost that time!"

It's nine in the morning. How could it be time for cake? The party isn't supposed to start until eleven.

"I have friends coming, Mama! Won't they want cake too?" Gracie asked, concerned as well.

"No, no, you see, I bought this cake special this year so we could enjoy it together first without anyone else," Naomi reassured her with a strained smile.

I was shocked. "So, I will be joining you after all then," I half said for Gracie's benefit, half for Naomi's.

Naomi scowled in return. "Um, if you're not busy. Gracie's seventh birthday is important, and we need to start it off with cake, right, baby girl?"

Gracie wasn't going to refuse a Barbie cake for breakfast. She squealed, flinging her arms in the air and yellow paint on the white shiplap wall.

6

WHEN WE CRESCENDOED

———

Paint spattered the wall like mustard squeezed onto white bread. It took me one sponge, four paper towels, and eight squirts of Windex to clear the yellow smear. One swipe would've been fine if it weren't for the stare of an extremely displeased Naomi above me.

The paint had misted on the walnut floor, even. My tendons screamed while on all fours, cleaning the wood. Once all was spotless and Naomi approved, I hoisted myself from the ground using an easel stool as an assistant. I crumpled the dirty wad of paper towels in my palm.

"So, what's so special about a seventh birthday?" I asked Naomi, shuffling past her to search for a trash can.

"I knew you'd ask that. Why wouldn't it be special?" Her hands fisted to her hips.

The stammer was odd for her, but I ignored it. Instead I spotted a short metal bucket sitting beside Naomi's desk. I catapulted my rubbish from afar, missing the rim. I could almost feel the eye roll circling in her sockets.

"Well, I feel like every birthday is special, right?" I asked while bending over to pick up the rubbish. My eyes watered a bit with the gravity. "Why is this one so different that we're eating cake without the guests? And why am I invited? Normally I'm not, because you resent me, or whatever."

I chucked the rubbish in the bucket and smelled the graphite from Naomi's latest work on the desk. I leaned in closer to the drawing, noticing that the woman was shedding a tear and pushing herself away from the man cradling her.

Such a happy reflection of us.

"Do you want a lie or the truth, Ben?"

Confused, I bounced my eyes to Naomi, her face flush with the equivalent of a pot of water beginning to bubble furiously beneath a lid. My gut twisted.

Why are we even arguing?

"Give me a lie, why don't cha?" I snapped, the sarcasm dripping from my tongue. I was sure to regret that.

Here comes the rolling boil.

A moan crescendoed into a scream that shredded my ears. "I think it's time you know, Ben!" she roared, then chomped her teeth together.

I could hear Gracie whispering to Jack in the kitchen even from up here. I used my hands to motion Naomi to lower her voice.

"I think you should be careful what you yell, Naomi. Gracie is probably listening."

"I don't care anymore, Ben! I really, really couldn't care less, in fact," she managed through gritted teeth. "My little girl already hates me because of you," she pointed at me. "She already thinks I don't love you, Ben. And you know what—she's right!"

Well, like I didn't know that all-fucking-ready.

She continued, "I loved the hell out of you when you were *you*. But this . . . this isn't doing it for me anymore. You're distant"—she moved closer to me—"you're uninteresting"—and closer—"and all you want to do is smoke." She jabbed my jean pocket, pushing me a step back against the desk.

"I think that's all a bit unfair," I said calmly, touching her hand on my thigh. "You understand how hard it is to quit."

"Yeah," she snickered, "well, I succeeded, and let me tell you, it's much easier than quitting this relationship. We've been together for so long, I always find myself coming back to you. But I think this is it for me. You haven't loved me since your injury. That's just the cold, hard truth I'm just now willing to accept."

Naomi rescued her hand from my touch and took two steps backward, out of my reach.

"Oh yeah, what the *fuck* is that supposed to mean, huh?" I crossed my arms to appear more in control than I felt. I didn't normally swear at her. I could tell my harsh words were a hornet stinging her skin. Naomi's shoulders pinched upward and her forehead vein throbbed enough to become noticeable.

"What did you just say to me?" she asked softly.

Here we go.

"I said what the *fuck* do you mean, this is it for you?" I wasn't backing down.

Naomi grabbed her ring finger, where a gold-and-emerald band hugged her skin. I gifted it to her a few Christmases ago.

"It means I think I'm fucking done. Hand to God, you bastard."

Naomi tugged the ring until it surrendered its resistance. She slipped it off, leaned past me, and dropped it into a cup of old paint water resting on the desk. The ring echoed like a tiny pebble dropping into an April puddle. My eyebrows furrowed. It took two years of sales at Marmo's to close that loan.

"I'm sure you didn't mean to do that, did you?" I dared, glaring at Naomi beneath my brows.

"Yes. I meant every second of that ring sinking to the bottom. Every second!" she screamed.

I grabbed the cup and dumped it on top of the desk and over her drawing, mostly out of spite. The water flooded the paper's fibers, erasing strokes of Naomi's time spent on the sad scene.

Naomi froze with neither a scream nor a word of blasphemy. Water spread over the paper, flowed over the glass desk's ledges, and dripped onto the floor. The ring settled over the blank breast of what was once a weeping woman.

7

INTO LITTLE, SMOKELESS FIRES.

———

Naomi glared at me with bloodshot eyes, clutching sopping paper towels in her hands. There was no chance of salvaging her work, though she tried mopping up what she could. The art melted in her hands as she stood.

"Are you happy now?" she muttered.

Ironic, isn't it? She failed to save a drawing that clearly depicted a broken relationship. Karma finds a way.

"Not as happy as you were taking that ring off your finger," I replied firmly.

Serves you right.

Naomi fell to the wet floor again at my feet, grabbed my legs, and sobbed. It surprised me, as she was usually a pretty sturdy woman.

I'm not sure I've ever seen her like this.

I stared at what I'm told used to be the love of my life— fingernails raw from anxious biting, orange paint somehow dried behind an ear—I couldn't remember how it felt to be in love with this human. I think it'd hurt more now if I did.

A minute or so passed before I knelt on the wooden floor to hold Naomi, my arms a barrier holding her above the floor. Her arms hugged me tightly. She collapsed her weight into my chest and buried her face in the crook of my elbow. I stroked her hair. It must've been cut just a few days ago. I caught the scent of the shampoo-like gel they used to keep her hair from frizzing. She always knew I liked that smell.

I'm not sure if I should say it . . .

"You know, if you want to leave me, you can always come back."

A muffled sniffle escaped from her nose, pulling the skin of the crook of my arm to her nostrils for a millisecond, long enough for me to notice the suction. Goosebumps ascended my arms and reminded me how much I missed the warmth of being touched.

I continued, "I say you can come back . . . because you're the only person I've ever wanted. Period. I'm certain of that." I paused. "Before my accident, you were the only thought on my mind—I'd be in the boonies in the middle of a desert with the possibility of being put away at any time, and I know my final thought would've been something about you. When the bomb exploded out there, even when my ears were ringing and I was lying in the sand and everything that fell to the earth around me was on fire, I saw you with me. Then I closed my eyes and woke up in a bed with practically a clean slate for a brain. I was still me . . . I knew who I was. I remembered my parents and Marmo's. I remembered Red. But anything else that was important to me vanished. One of those things was you. I didn't ask for this, and I'd change it if I could."

Damn, I've never said anything like that out loud . . .

Talking about that day made my brain flash into a swell of rapid, black-and-white memories.

The young man ran across a sandy path. A sack leaked in his hand and he held a lit cigarette in the other. My buddy, Eddie, yelled at him to get back . . .

Naomi mumbled something in my arm that brought me to the present, but I couldn't quite make out what she uttered. I thought I caught a faint, "I'm sorry."

"Can you say that again?" I asked, staring at her from above.

She lifted her head from my arm and focused her gaze on the wall. "I'm sorry. I'm sorry for everything that happened," she admitted, shifting her body to lay her head on my thighs so she could peer into my eyes. "But even if all of that is true, it doesn't . . . make up for any of what you've put me through. The forgetting . . . the forgetting slowly stripped you away from me in a way I didn't know how to help. You somehow had to try and refall in love with a stranger, and I somehow had to continue giving my heart to someone who was no longer in love with me. Even after all of these years, we just aren't the same."

She put her hands over her face and cried. "It's harsh, Ben, I know it," she wailed in her hands. "I just don't want any part of this loveless life anymore."

I looked around the room at all of the faded lovers and put a wet, unraveled strand of Naomi's hair behind her ear. "I told you if you wanted to leave, you're welcome back when you're ready, babe."

Naomi uncovered her face, revealing flushed cheeks and a red nose. Her eyes remained squeezed shut as she adjusted to a cross-legged position in front of me. When her legs were aligned, she lifted her eyelids slowly, revealing those evergreen eyes. Coolly she asked, "Do you want me to leave?"

My eyes scanned the ink renditions of our relationship hanging on the walls around us. A couple sleeping on opposite sides of the bed, the same couple riding in a car without holding hands, a slew of smudged half-smiles plastered on the wall here and there.

How can I feel such compassion for someone and dislike them so much at the same time?

I shifted into a cross-legged position myself, groaning with the movement of my creaking joints.

"No, I don't really want you to leave . . ." I sighed. "But I'm also not certain what I want. I think I'm afraid of what I'm already missing and don't want to see you hang on if you don't have to."

Naomi's lower lip trembled. "I've thought about it time and time again, and I think I'd like to go, but I'm worried what that might do to you."

What it might do to me? Really?

"Why even care about me, Naomi? If going will make you happy, you should go." I pointed at the door. "It's that simple."

"Yeah, you think it's that easy?" she sniffled. "To just disappear out of your life? I'd love to just disappear . . ." she trailed off. "I thought I could bring you back, Ben." She choked up again. "I don't think I can bring you back, and that hurts more than anything."

Naomi slanted her torso forward and hugged me again. Her shoulders shook, pulsating a sadness throughout her entire body. I could feel it vibrating my own.

She continued, "The sad thing is I think you'll never remember the *us* that really existed before your accident. We had an inseparable, crazy kind of love. The kind that people would notice when you went to the movies or to a restaurant and someone would whisper to their friend, 'Ah, now *they* are in love.'" She pressed her forehead down upon my shoulder. "At least I'm aware of what and who I'm leaving.

But you—you will have absolutely no idea what you'll be missing when I'm gone."

She's right.

I was never more convinced about anything, ever. That was the reason she hung on so tightly. She was afraid to be forgotten after trying so hard to be remembered.

My hamstrings tugged when I leaned in to kiss Naomi's forehead. I wondered if it would be for the last time.

"Darling," I whispered, "I think you need to decide what will light your fire again."

8

DENIAL DISROBES
ME STILL—

———

My arms locked Naomi in a hug that felt void of consolation. We were both intermittently sponging our moist eyes with our wrists. While I was mid-sniffle, Gracie yelled up to us from below.

"Mama! Daddy! Whatcha doin'?"

Oh my God—what are we going to tell Gracie?

My face felt numb. Actually, my entire being felt like it'd been soaked in anesthesia, including my heart. Naomi peeled away from me and scrambled up first. To my surprise, she fetched my cane and tugged me up with the might of her forearms.

"I suppose this is it, then?" I asked her faintly. I recalled what I told Naomi all those years ago:

"Promise me, for your own sake, you'll leave if you feel like I've become a stranger to you too." Goddammit, why the fuck would I ask her to promise something like that?

I rested my palm on Naomi's shoulder, trying to summon an answer. I could tell from her forlorn, lost face that she had made up her mind. Shivering, she nodded.

I was never going to be able to give that spark back to her. I couldn't even find my own.

A world without Naomi in it may have been created for me by accident, but she had always been there waiting nonetheless. I was petrified.

The room swirled with the phases of our lives looking down at us.

I might need that wastebasket again.

I carefully lifted my hand from Naomi and edged a few inches backward toward her desk in case I couldn't hold things together. I continued facing her. "So, where do we go from here? What happens to you? To us? And Gracie?" I questioned the dewy-eyed woman of mine. Or *former* woman of mine.

A soft thud came from downstairs that sounded like Gracie getting into the fridge for a swig of juice.

Naomi rubbed her eyes with her knuckles and shrugged. "Well, there's not much of *us* left, babe. But I'm going to go find my spark. I'm going to go away for a while, maybe a long while, and try to clear my head," she declared. "Someday maybe you'll look into a crowd and spot me. Maybe you'll feel something then."

The venom in those last few words stung my chest, but I felt less nauseous knowing she wouldn't take Gracie from me. I wondered at her satisfaction in making me feel inferior, even now.

"I'd change the outcome if I could." I wiped some wet from my mouth. "I'm not going to kick my feet and scream. I did the best I could do, and I can't keep you here if you don't wanna stay."

I leaned forward to envelop Naomi in a side hug, but she cringed and took a step back. She bent to wipe her palms on her ripped, blue painting jeans. She was still shivering.

"Okay . . ." I paused at her rejection and shoved my hand in my pocket instead.

Damn, that cigarette feels nice.

"Mama? Dad?" Gracie called from below.

"Just a minute, sweetheart," Naomi called. "Your father and I are talking."

I lowered my voice to a whisper. "So . . . what are we going to do about Gracie? She's going to wonder where you've gone. You're really just going to disappear out of her life, too? Do you want to build a schedule or something?"

Naomi huffed at the thought and pulled a strand of loose, salty hair behind her ear.

"I don't think that's such a good idea, Ben. I'd like a little more peace while I find some clarity . . . you can handle her until I return. She loves you."

Oh, and when will that be?

I still felt like I was submerged in a room that mimicked my first time riding a merry-go-round at the county fair.

"So what, you're just going to leave both of us? Gracie too?" My arms flailed in the air as I wasted my breath, repeating what I already knew.

Naomi's face flamed. "You know very damn well I was never meant to have her with you, Ben," she bit through clenched teeth. "My Grace was supposed to be born with someone I love that loves me back. This wasn't meant to happen with you like this."

The words needled into my face.

"Just because she wasn't in your grand plan doesn't mean you can just fucking forgo being a mother. I mean, what the hell, Naomi. Do you hear yourself? Listen to yourself. You're acting crazy."

I wish I could shake her to wake her up from insanity.

"It doesn't seem so crazy to me . . . I love Gracie so much," she lamented, resting a hand on her chest. "But even with all the love I have for her, I feel like my absence will be better for you and her both. I'm trying to avoid being selfish. I just don't think you understand that selflessness."

Do. Not. Shake. Her.

I crossed my arms. "I'm sorry—but selflessness is not what this is. This is stupidity. You're being foolish and you know it. You're just trying to hide under a rock so you can forget any life you had with me."

Discomfort mingled with the smell of dust and paint in the room. Naomi twisted her upper body toward the room's entrance and yelled, "Hey sweetie, Mama and Dad are coming down, okay?" She pivoted back to me and firmly said, "I'm done with this, Ben. Trust me, you can handle her."

I enjoyed seeing Naomi's hair bun bounce as she left the room and disappeared down the stairs, perhaps for the last time. Our daughter chattered on and on to her about little ole Jack and the Barbie cake. I tried to gather my composure for whatever was going to happen next. I touched a hand to my pocket.

Goddamn it, I need a smoke.

I forced my hand away and leaned deeper into my cane instead.

I'll need at least an entire pack later.

My eyes darted around the room at all of the lovers. I sighed and tottered to the stairs' landing. I eavesdropped on Naomi and Gracie's conversation from above.

"I think you, Jack, and Daddy should take the cake to the shop and celebrate today since your friends all want to celebrate at the park another day," Naomi said, hugging Gracie and rubbing her back.

I guess her friends weren't really invited.

"Oh, that sounds nice, Mama! Aren't you coming to the shop too?"

Naomi released her embrace, stared into Gracie's eyes, and softly stated, "Mama's gotta' pack."

"Why? Oh, are you going on a fishing trip too?" Gracie asked excitedly.

"Somethin' like that, doll," Naomi replied, giving her another squeeze.

Gracie didn't ask any more questions. Her eyes darted up to me on the staircase.

"Well, to the shop we go!" I said with as much enthusiasm as I could. "Go change and get in Red with Jack and I'll grab the cake for us."

Gracie raced to her room down the hall to change into a pink sequined dress with purple cotton leggings. As she zipped past me when I finally reached the kitchen, I could have mistaken her for a mermaid with legs.

I let out an honest chuckle about her outfit choice. "Whoa, whoa, whoa, where's your birthday crown this year?" I asked, halting her mid-step past me. She always chose to wear a bedazzled plastic crown for her birthday.

"Seven is for big girls. Big girls don't need crowns," Gracie sassed.

Seven's going to be interesting.

Naomi scooped Gracie up and twirled her in a circle around the kitchen. The fake smile curving from her lips for our daughter's sake made me wince.

I probably won't witness this dance ever again.

"You *are* a big girl!" Naomi yelled, fueling Gracie's shrieking laughter. She slowed her twirl, set her down, and bowed her head for a special kiss from Grace.

With a final peck on her mom's forehead, Gracie spun around and spurted out the screen door.

Naomi straightened and opened a drawer to grab some Saran Wrap. She faced the counter, wrapping the gaudy, pink cake. A sugary, magenta gumdrop slipped onto the countertop in the process, along with several tears. I touched her shoulder softly from behind as an olive branch. She shrank from my reach.

"Please know you can come back any time, babe," I reiterated. Her empty gaze remained on the cabinet in front of her as she held out the cake.

"I'm sure you'll be standing with open arms," she jabbed without making eye contact.

"Maybe. Maybe not," I said. "But you know who will be."

I snatched the cake, kissed her neck, and slammed the door on my way out.

9

THE TAPESTRY UNDONE
AND EXPOSED;

———

It took me several minutes to jiggle the doorknob open to Marmo's. Finally, the right notch of the key caught the innards of the lock and I swung into the front entrance. Layers of overwhelming dust filled my nostrils. The red-and-blue ornaments dangled out of place as I entered the threshold. Gracie trailed behind me at first, then dashed to the bay window.

"Cake time, cake time, cake time," she sang, already bouncing in her pillowed alcove on the wooden sill.

"Alright now, settle down a minute," I laughed, balancing the dessert and examining the cashier's counter from afar.

Do I even have silverware?

I hadn't been in to sell or craft anything in the store for weeks. Handwritten orders for chess pieces, dinner plates, and custom liquor bottles sat on the counter beneath a paperweight I made when I was twelve, maybe. It'd been a long time since I thought about such things.

The rubber stop on my cane tapped the floor as I headed in the direction of work, but Gracie darted up from her spot and launched in front of me before I could take one step. She halted me by raising one meager, yellow-tinted hand in front of my chest.

"Ben, I'd really, pretty please, love something to eat. We haven't had anything *all day*, and I'm seven!"

My eyebrows raised in shock at the use of my first name. She'd never said it before. At least not directly to me.

"Uh—baby girl, why are you calling me 'Ben' all of a sudden?" I asked, following Gracie's hand as it lowered to her side.

"I don't know, I heard it from Mama at home and it feels . . . right."

Oh no, she was listening.

I laughed, nervously. "Well, you're not wrong. That is the name that your ole Pa gave me."

Rest his soul.

"You can just call me Daddy. Mama calls me Ben because she likes the way it sounds," I fudged.

"Why?" she questioned.

Yeah, Ben. Why?

"Uh, because that's what she called me when she and I first met a long time ago. It makes her . . . happy." My throat clogged at the thought of having to talk to Gracie about Naomi. I let out a cough that felt like pennies scraping cold butter.

"Why does Mama sound so upset when she's calling you that, then?" Gracie pressed on.

How am I gonna do this?

"Uh, because, sweetie, sometimes anger is confused for love. Sometimes when we sound upset it's because we are expressing to someone how much they mean to us with our voice."

"Oh, I guess that makes sense, Daddy," she uttered to my relief, wandering back over to her sunny niche. My shoulders eased with the interrogation over. I briefly contemplated foraging for silverware in the counter's drawers, but instead limped to the bay window. I plopped down next to Gracie and her now blinding, shimmering sequin dress.

"Man, I need to wrap you up in a blanket, doll. I can't see a thing!" I held a hand over my squinting eyes, the pink sequins splitting into a thousand tiny beams.

Gracie quickly exclaimed, "It's okay, I can do it!" She took the cake from my hands, set it on the windowsill, and peeled off the Saran Wrap. Half of the frosting peeled away with it. The once-beautiful cake, now undone and exposed, revealed its ugly layers beneath.

"Any plates?" she asked.

"We don't have any utensils or plates, so we'll just have to pick it up like pizza," I muffled, peering through one hand's peephole. I crumbled a chunk of cake in my other hand and shoved a bite of the dewy, yellow base in my mouth.

"That's fine, Daddy," she assured. She scooped her finger into a blob of what pink frosting remained, stuck out her tongue, and licked her finger.

Gracie was satisfied playing with and eating her birthday cake for a while. I interrupted several minutes of silence.

"I'm sorry I have no birthday candles for ya this year, sweetie. But I do have a spare match for you to make a wish." I heaved myself up and hobbled to the counter in search of the box of matches. I knew I'd shoved them somewhere to light my cigarettes in case my lighter were to break on some off chance.

Ah, there they are.

The matchbox was forced into a narrow drawer. I untucked it from beneath some papers and pulled a match from its lair.

I struck it on the coarse side of the box. The warm, orange light of fire glowed in my cupped hand.

"Make a wish," I drifted to Gracie with the flickering stick. She squeezed her eyes shut, drew a long breath, and puffed the match out just before it reached my thumb. I hoped the wish was for something I could give her.

"Happy seventh birthday, baby doll."

Gracie smiled, but I could sense sadness in her lowered eyes.

"Honey, what's wrong?" I asked.

"Nothing, Ben," she murmured.

Not this again.

"Hmm . . . baby girl, did you hear Mama and I talking earlier?"

"Maybe," she said quietly.

Here we go.

I ran a hand through my coarse beard—something I always did when I didn't have the right words at the right time.

"What did you hear?" I asked, reluctantly.

Gracie sat crisscross now with her elbows on her knees.

"Well . . . it sounded like you and Mama were yelling. And mad. And I heard Mama crying. She said that you could handle me. What does the word *handle* mean?"

My lungs felt heavy, though I already took medication for that. "Uh, well, it means I can take care of you well. I do that, don't I?"

"Yeah . . ." Gracie replied.

"So . . . what's the issue then, darling?" I asked.

"Mama's going to go away again. She always takes a vacation after you guys talk upstairs," Gracie said.

Well, she ain't wrong there.

I thought of a swift reply this time—something relatable to minimize the impact of this mess.

"Baby doll, I need you to hear me out on this for just a sec. You can have big girl talk now, right?"

"Yes, Dad, I *am* seven," Gracie mouthed.

"Okay, good. Well you're right, Mama is going on vacation for a while."

"For how long?" she asked, concerned.

"Well, see, here's the thing. Do you remember yesterday when you held the fish and you were sad that we kept it? And you cried over it?" I asked.

"Mm-hmm . . ."

"Okay, good. Well, if we had put the fish back in the water after we caught it, you wouldn't have been sad, right, and the fish would have been happy and swimming away?"

Her eyes flickered with the remembrance of our dinner. "Yeah—" Her words stumbled.

"Well your Mama is like that fish. Instead of us keeping her and having us be sad with her, she wants to be set free so she can be happy," I finished.

"Dad, we're not eating Mama, though," Gracie pointed out, wrinkling her nose.

Good point.

"No, we're not. But we are keeping her and holding on to her. And your Mama loves to swim. She's just like that fish. She wants to be let back out into the water so she can be happy. Sometimes letting go is the best thing to do."

Gracie furrowed her eyebrows, signifying her thinking face.

She eventually said, "I guess letting go is good, but I'm going to miss Mama. I wish she was less like the fish."

10

I LET OUR SNAGS
UNTANGLE

———

The whiskey teased my lips as I sipped from my metal pocket flask. I had picked up the habit since my wife's leaving, and that was almost two years ago now.

"Whoa, Gracie, *steady!*" I yelled at my hobbling daughter, who almost toppled our rental canoe into the Elk. I stabilized the boat by grabbing its sides with my free hand and shifting my weight with the current. Gracie gently sat down on the furthest plank opposite me and we reached our usual equilibrium.

"You can't be standing up so all of a sudden to look at the fish," I remarked.

"Sorry, Dad, I know. I just got excited because I thought I saw a big one," she muttered, slumping her shoulders.

My girl had changed a lot in the last couple of years. Her blonde hair had faded into a soft brunette, she started swiping her bangs to the side of her face rather than over her brows, and she had somehow managed to spurt several inches in height. She had also replaced pink with turquoise as her new favorite color, found worms repulsive, and talked much, much less. The talking diminished after her mom didn't make a return on her eighth birthday.

"Oh, you think you saw one, huh? Whereabouts?" I asked.

Gracie pointed about five feet out. "We like 'em when they're that close. Easy targets," I commented, not anticipating much of a reply. I prepped the line of my standard rod for a short cast.

The annual trip to the Elk was much needed this year. More than most. We didn't make it out last August for Gracie's birthday for the first time since she was a newborn because she insisted on remaining inside Naomi's art room in case she was to come home. I hadn't been up there since the day Naomi left, and quite honestly, if it weren't for Gracie nudging me to go in, I probably wouldn't have set foot in the room again. Alas, I inspected Naomi's ruined piece of us still adorning her desk and called those hazy, repressed memories to the forefront.

The stress made me chain-smoke, shoving Gracie out of the only place she wanted to be that day. She rebelled in response. She scooped up all of the nonperishable food she could from the kitchen pantry and quarantined herself in her bedroom for three days. The door only creaked open every few hours so she could tiptoe to the bathroom. Even then, she locked herself back up again five minutes later. On the morning of Gracie's third day of self-imposed seclusion, I gently tapped on her door and asked to talk. Of course she refrained from letting me in, so I used a butter knife to pick the lock. I never heard someone scream "Get out!" so fast in my life, not even over a walkie-talkie in battle. It took three bowls of chocolate ice cream with rainbow sprinkles and one sing-along Disney movie to get on good terms by the end of that evening.

Since that birthday, I had felt a disconnect between Gracie and me, especially as she got closer to being nine, yet another year older, at the end of this week. If anything could rewire our brains to default back to our comfortable father-daughter state, it'd be instances like these.

I launched my bobber to the heavens and relished its smooth free fall to the river's surface. Ripples diffused from its plunk and petered out before reaching us. Instead of indulging in any of it, Gracie picked at a piece of skin ripping from her cuticle.

"That hurt?" I nodded to her from the far end of the canoe.

"Yeah, it hurts. It's a hangnail," Gracie said emphatically.

"Okay . . ." My voice loitered as she struggled to tug it from her pinky. "Do you want to see a trick?" I asked. Her finger was flush from the prodding.

"Um, yes, actually," she replied, offering her hand up to me from afar. I pocketed my flask, surged forward from my end of the canoe, and teetered toward her.

I took Gracie's soft hand, she scooted to make room for me on the plank, and I sat beside her. "I learned this when I was about your age."

I rested her hand delicately on my kneecap. A spot of blood crept from where the hangnail plagued her with a persistent sting.

"Now, what you do is take the hangnail, softly, as to not hurt yourself . . . and twist it." I nipped the skin and lightly spun it ninety degrees. Gracie flinched but didn't cry out.

"Okay, but how does it rip off? Won't it hurt?" she asked.

I continued softly twisting the snag in circles. "Well, eventually, the end point gets so teeny tiny that it breaks off."

Gracie looked away so she didn't have to perceive what she thought was forecasted pain. Meanwhile, the hangnail detached, and I flicked it to our feet.

"Sweetie, it's gone," I said, to her surprise.

"Oh wow—that really worked, huh? I'm going to have to tell my friends that one!" she gushed, leaning in to inspect her pinky. I soaked in her relieved sentiment and my moment of hero status.

"I think they'd find it just as helpful. It's nice not to have to feel the pain," I stated.

Maybe this is a good time to talk fly fishing. It'll give us something more to chat about.

I continued, "Speaking of which, 'member that one summer I poked myself tryin' to tie my own fly?" I nudged her with my elbow.

Gracie laughed. "Dad, I was like, five when you did that. And yes, you were bleeding, like, everywhere!"

I snickered. "Yeah, I was, wasn't I . . ." I reflected before lunging to grab my knapsack resting in the middle of the canoe. The water splashed with the boat's sway. "Hey, so, I thought maybe you'd enjoy making your own flies this year." I rummaged in the front pocket for some old hooks I had torn apart, feathers, Sharpies, and hook thread I picked up from CVS the week before. I felt the needle-nose pliers first and set them on the boat's tin floor.

"Yeah! I'm not sure I'd be good at it, but it looked fun when you tried," she said, smirking at me.

I chuckled at her sarcasm. "Well, I've only done it a few times. You'll be fine . . . it's no different than beading a bracelet. Just takes lots of patience is all," I replied, still foraging for the hooks.

Jesus, you'd think I'd have bagged these things.

I felt a poke.

Gotcha.

I clutched one of the number six hooks, located the rest of the necessities, and took my time rotating around and adjusting my body to the floor.

Right there would be just fine.

I shifted our crafting materials to my lap and surrendered the pliers. "Do you remember what we do first?" I asked her, wiping a bead of sweat from my tanned brow, a gift from the record-setting humidity that day.

"Hmm . . . I don't think so. Maybe cut up some feathers?" she answered.

"Ah, see, you *do* remember that!" I tossed the white feathers up on the plank.

Gracie replaced the pliers with the bag of feathers and tore them open. One of the smallest ones ejected from the pack and swirled into the sky. Only seconds passed until a barn swallow swooped down to snatch the new addition to its nest. We gawked at its swiftness.

"I always liked those birds," Gracie commented. She took out a feather of her own and pressed it between her knees. "I'm gonna need your knife to cut this."

I dug for my pocketknife and surrendered it to Gracie. She pried it open and sawed at the stem until a half-inch piece split off.

"Attagirl!" I cheered. "Alright, now we need to tie that thing onto this." I squeezed the hook between my thumb and pointer finger and raised it to Gracie's eye level. "If you do the tying, I'll do the holding."

"Only if you don't poke yourself this time," she teased. She picked up the black thread at my feet, untwined it from its cardboard, and snipped off a long line.

I used two hands to hold the hook, sharp ends toward me, so Gracie could twine the feather around the base. She aligned the feather, which I secured with my thumbs, and began wrapping.

"This doesn't seem so hard this time," she said, circling the thread around and around.

"Sometimes it takes a village to build a barn, baby girl," I smiled. The last time I'd attempted fly making, I'd rushed the process terribly, fighting the clock since the trout were already biting. "Make sure to move the thread all the way up the base."

She's way more patient with this than I ever was.

I fixated on Gracie's nimble hands twirling and then pooled my spiraling eyes on the Elk. The water swirled with my dizziness. After several minutes, Gracie's spin slowed from fatigue.

"How much longer, Dad?"

"Patience, my dear," I replied, plummeting from space to scan her work.

This is good practice for both of us.

"Eh, I think that'll do great," I affirmed. "Now, for varnish. Hold this."

Gracie seized the hook I placed in her lap while I reached into the knapsack.

"Just a dab, alright? I'll let you handle it," I said, still foraging.

Handle it. That word felt familiar.

I unearthed the nail polish from the bottom of my bag and passed it on. Gracie dripped a glob of polish onto the string.

Ah, fuck.

"Oops!" she exclaimed, clenching her teeth.

"It's okay, it's okay, lemme just . . . here," I retrieved the hook, wiped away the stickiness with one of my bandanas, and sent it back. "Let's try that again."

Gracie cradled the hook in her hands and smudged a dot onto the ends of the thread.

"Much better, baby girl," I approved. "See what a difference patience makes?"

She nodded. "Can I color it now?" she asked eagerly.

That's still her favorite part, huh?

"Yes, it's about that time. Pick a light color," I flashed her some options. She chose the turquoise marker, as I had anticipated.

Gracie hunched over her bare thighs at what was starting to resemble a proper fly. She tinted the feather's fibers, shading the left strands, then the right. I encouraged her to add some black speckles since the trout around the Elk liked patterns.

Maybe that's just in my head.

While Gracie focused on her art, I scooted forward and comfortably put my feet up next to her. I leaned my back on the nearest plank and removed my green fishing cap from my head, planting it over my face.

Ah, nothing like a lucky cap.

The chirping swallows and smell of blackberries on the shore lulled me to sleep despite the blazing sun.

"Hey, Dad?" Gracie's muffled voice entered the quiet space beneath my hat.

How long have I been asleep?

I yawned, disinclined to remove myself from my snug darkness. "Yeah, sweetie?"

"That was fun. Can I try to make one on my own? I promise I'll be patient."

"Um, sure, I don't see why not. Just don't poke yourself," I said jokingly.

I drifted back into the twilight zone of my nap when Gracie tapped my foot.

"Huh—yeah?" I jolted. "I'm awake."

"Dad?" Gracie asked.

"Yeah, babe?"

"This is a really great birthday."

11

TO VOW A NEW THREAD.

———

I tugged a few gray hairs from my still mostly dark beard in Red's rearview mirror. I was getting a lot of those lately, especially because Gracie was going to enter middle school and start sixth grade in a few weeks.

Yikes, I'm getting old.

Gracie waved goodbye to the neighbor boys from the passenger seat as I put the car in reverse and backed out of the driveway. I leaned forward and scowled at the two eleven-year-olds standing in our yard. Their eyes enlarged with my entry into their nonverbal conversation.

Yeah, that's right, you better be scared.

Gracie spun around and slapped my shoulder when she realized what I was doing.

"Dad, you're, like, so embarrassing sometimes," she groaned.

Gracie's face and body had matured. She refused to cut her hair since she turned ten and let it grow down to her lower back, though she always wore it in a loose French braid after her best friend, Ava, taught her how at a recent sleepover. She had grown increasingly more conscious of things like deodorant and shaving her legs since joining the local youth group's soccer squad, or team, or whatever they referred to themselves as. Oh, and she preferred to be called just "Grace" because she thought of herself as an "adult now."

I braked for a passing car and held up a hand in defense for my supposed wrongdoing. "Hey, sorry cupcake, but I gotta show those gentlemen who's who here."

"Ew, you're gross! Luca and Miles are just friends. Period," she sassed.

"Trust me, I wasn't suggesting otherwise!"

I put the car in drive, shot down the road, and drove through the Clarksburg suburbs to reach the thruway. I set Red on cruise control at seventy-two miles per hour. The one-hour push to our parking spot at the Sutton Dam would need all the attention I had for Gracie's benefit. I even twisted the radio knob off out of nervousness, though it hadn't worked in years.

"So, Mr. Zhao phoned me last night . . ." I said, uncanning a potentially difficult conversation. Mr. Zhao taught seventh grade science at the Clarksburg middle school and coached her youth soccer team.

"Oh? And what's he doing calling you on a Friday night?" she questioned, her eyes aimed straight forward. "We don't have a tournament this weekend or anything."

I know she knows why.

I bit my lower lip. Then released. "Well, he mentioned how some girls might be treating you unfairly and pushin' you on the ground at practice."

"Oh? You mean what Frankie did last week?" she fronted.

Yeah, that little brat, Francesca.

"Right, what Frankie did. She shouldn't be shoving you to the ground. Is she mean to you all the time like that?"

Francesca and Gracie started off fifth grade as friends. Then, from what I heard through the grapevine that is parenthood, Francesca was playing with older kids on the weekends. Like, seventh graders. Then she'd come over to the house and start making fun of Gracie for wanting to play with dolls, or for not painting her nails, or for still having a stuffed animal sitting on her bed. It pissed me right off.

"No, Dad, only sometimes," Gracie replied. "She was just pretending to be cool. She helped me up afterward."

I fumed silently before acknowledging her optimism. Trees whizzed by us on both sides.

"You know, you don't have to be friends with her, Gracie."

Gracie put her feet on the dashboard, leaned the car seat back, and closed her eyes. The car was packed with buckets, bags, and coolers as usual, so she didn't back too far out of my peripheral.

"I'm not tryin' to pester you. Again, all I'm saying is you don't have to be friends with her, Gracie. Having friends is important, but they should never hurt you on purpose—especially if they're just trying to look cool."

She cranked the window all the way down to signify she didn't want to talk about it. The air whipped chunks of hair that had been stuffed in a braid. The remainder of the car ride to the Elk was silent, filled only with the rush of wind slapping our eardrums and me biting my tongue.

Gracie nodded awake when Red rumbled through the gravel drive. I parked in our usual spot on top of the hill that overlooked the Elk. I let out a long-winded exhale thanks to the medications I was still picking up from Ms. Mia at the pharmacy.

I placed a hand on Gracie's shoulder. "We're here."

"Clearly," she sputtered while rolling up the window. The clouds furled above, appearing as angry as the stormy pout on my daughter's face.

"Okay now . . . what—you're going to be mad at me because I brought up Francesca?" I asked.

"Her name is Frankie, and no, I'm not." Her furrowed brow expressed otherwise.

"I just want you to be happy, Gracie. I didn't want to bring it up in the first place, but when Mr. Zhao called, I was pretty alarmed that even *he* thought I should know about it." I sounded defensive, but my tone also could've been mistaken for aggravation.

She rolled her eyes at me. "I'm going for a walk," she stated and opened the car door. Before it shut, she added, "Oh, and I told you to call me Grace."

My knee almost buckled with the speed in which I opened the door to yell after her.

"Oh yeah, you're going to run off with this rain coming, huh?" The hurt in my chest vibrated, my voice an echo in the trees chasing after my seething daughter.

I whipped out a cigarette from my flannel for consolation. While lighting it in the drive, a water droplet fell on my nose. *What did I say wrong?*

It poured for almost two hours before Gracie knocked on the driver's side window to be let in. Her hoodie had transformed from a lilac to a deep purple and the hood of it was tightly squeezed around her face. She knocked again.

"Dad, unlock the doors, I'm freezing."

I could hear her chattering teeth from inside. I flipped the lock from the door behind me and Gracie shoved whatever shit she could to the floor that prevented her from sitting comfortably.

"I don't think . . . it's ever rained on our fishing trip before." She trembled.

"Yeah, I think you're right about that." Sounds of warming up came from the back seat—Gracie's hands chafed together and air from her lungs huffed into the cave she made around her mouth. "Ya hungry?" I asked.

"I am. What're we gonna eat? I'm not really in the mood for snacks. I was craving fresh fish."

I spun around. "Well, here are your options. We can drive twenty minutes north to the nearest 7-Eleven for some pizza. Or . . ."

"Or?" she asked.

"Or . . . we can go thirty minutes east to Pete's Diner."

She perked up at that. "Oh hell yeah, let's go to Pete's! I forgot about that place."

I circled back to face the wheel and smiled. "Alright, Pete's it is. But you can only get a slice of cherry pie for dessert if you mind your language, little lady." I ignited Red and we rolled out of the gravel drive.

Gracie chatted endlessly during the ride to Pete's. She talked about things that were well out of my league: iPhones that her classmates had, liquid eyeliner that *all* the girls at practice were wearing, what glittery Five Star notebook she "absolutely needed" for her school notes, and how Ava's oldest sister just had her first kiss. By the time I pulled into Pete's, I was exhausted.

We waltzed into the dirt-old, neon-lit diner just in time for their dinner specials. It was the only sit-down restaurant in that town.

"Why don't you read the specials chalkboard and grab a booth while I use the restroom?" I asked. I needed to splash some water on my face to wake up from all the talking.

"On it!" she exclaimed.

I shuffled in and out of the family bathroom pretty quickly—fast enough to have caught the red-haired waitress laughing at something Gracie was saying.

"Ah, there he is," Gracie said, pointing at me.

I raised my eyebrows.

"Here I am!" I reiterated, sliding into the red leather seat across from Gracie. "What's the scoop?"

"The waitress said that I was cute. I told her that if she thought I was cute, she should meet my father." Gracie giggled.

The waitress blushed. So did I.

"Kids. Amiright?" I taunted while shaking my head, admiring the woman's kind smile.

"Oh yes, I have one of my own. They sure do keep you on your toes," she agreed. She jotted something on the pad in her hand and escaped to grab waters.

I took note that she wasn't wearing a wedding ring. Not that one signified much these days.

"What was that all about?" I asked.

Gracie said, "Well since Mama isn't coming back, I just thought I'd introduce you."

My eyebrows shot to the sky.

"Do you know her?" I asked.

"No," Gracie mused, "but she seems nice. Her name is Gabriella. I read it on her name tag."

I was uncertain whether to feel endeared or anxious that my daughter was scoping out someone on my behalf. I was eager to put the theory that I was on the hunt for a relationship behind us when Gabriella returned with two plastic, Pepsi-branded cups.

"Can I take your orders?" she asked, nodding at Gracie first. Her gentle southern voice poured into my ears like honey.

"I'd like the haddock fish fry with coleslaw and fries, please ma'am," Gracie requested.

"And you?" Gabriella pointed her pen at me.

"On my end, I'll have a steak, medium-rare, with fries."

She jotted our items on her notepad and swirled off to tell the cook, swinging her hips noticeably. "That'll be right up," she yelled without looking back.

I nonchalantly stared in her direction longer than I should've, smirked, then wheeled my focus back to my smiling daughter.

Maybe now's a good time to bring back those growing pains.

"Sweetie—" I started, pulling a brown napkin out of the dispenser on the table. "I need ya to hear me out on somethin'."

"Okay . . . ?" Gracie responded, her smile fading.

"I'm going to draw you somethin' on here and I'm going to ask you what you think it means. 'Kay?"

I reached for the plastic cup next to the salt and pepper and dumped some Crayola's onto the table. I snatched Blue-Green and started sketching what I thought the Elk would look like from underwater. I scribbled a solid river bottom, some stringy submerged plants, a couple circular and inaccurate boulders, a bunch of triangular trout swimming downstream, and one swimming up.

Well, I fuckin' should practice this more often. Clearly.

"So, what do you think it means?" I pinched the napkin's corners and held it up. All I could smell was wax while Gracie inspected the piece of work.

"Uh, fish swim in one direction mainly?" she asked.

I poked my nose over the napkin edge to reevaluate my handiwork and shook my head.

"Guess again, sugar."

"Hmm . . . it's okay to be by yourself?" she asked, closer this time.

I shook my head again. "Not quite, a bit cliché, but warmer . . ."

Gabriella interrupted us by placing a basket of rolls and butter on the table, though her presence didn't interrupt me this time. I gazed through her slim body at my confused and quiet daughter and didn't look when she strutted away.

"Well, if you give up . . . it's supposed to mean that it's okay to swim away sometimes. You know what's actually downstream?" I flipped the napkin around, drew an admittedly shaky line into the water, and added a hook at its end above the school of trout. "Sometimes you can't predict what's downstream. But in this case, it's a hook."

"Uh-huh, and—?" she asked.

"Well, sometimes if you stick around those who are no good for you, you start to get caught in a current that can lead you into some pretty dangerous situations. If you can spot that beforehand, and you choose to swim away, you will avoid a lot of trouble and your life will be much better off."

I hope this is making sense.

"Oh, I see," Gracie stated with realization. "So if I'm connecting dots right, you're saying that Frankie is no good for me and I should be avoiding her?"

I read about this preteen drama shit somewhere. Let's play this safe.

"I'm not saying Frankie is bad for you. But what I *am* saying is that you should recognize when it's the right time to go your own way—whether being pushed on the soccer field, running for president, finding the perfect patch of stream, or otherwise."

Gracie stared blankly at me but nodded in confirmation. She was less annoyed than anticipated with the analogy, especially compared to her reaction to the conversation earlier.

I crumpled the napkin with one hand and stuffed it in the Crayola cup. We sat without conversation for twenty minutes before Gabriella plopped two white, plastic platters of food in front of us both.

"Bon appétit!" she called out, winking at me as she whirled away. Her hips swung more wildly each time she left the table. In the midst of another quick and covert gawk at Gabriella, I noted in my peripheral that Gracie grabbed my crumpled artwork, kissed it, and shoved it in her hoodie pocket.

"Oh, you want to keep that, aye?" I asked her jokingly, making eye contact while pitching a forkful of steak in my mouth.

Her face rouged at being caught.

"Oh, you know, just trying to soak in all this fishing knowledge . . . I've got a helluva lot to learn."

12

YOU HAD A SKINNY LOVE THEN,

———

Something happened to my sweet daughter not long after Ava's parents suggested I get Gracie a cell phone for her twelfth birthday.

After all, you should want to keep in contact with Gracie as much as possible, I mocked Ava's mom, Rosalie, in my head.

As much as I thought that Ava's mom and dad were the gods of Helicopter Parenting, they convinced me that being able to keep tabs on my daughter after school wasn't a bad idea.

Wouldn't want her hanging out with the wrong crowd and not knowing how to contact her, their words echoed.

Two months before Gracie turned twelve, I drove to Clarksburg's local tech shop and paid $800 for the "best phone on the market," as promised by a middle-aged guy in a seemingly decent suit. He popped the device in its shiny product box, slipped it into a bag, and handed the thing over. That was the last time I saw it before Gracie's birthday.

After the squealing and hopping up and down finally dwindled upon Gracie's opening of the gleaming package,

I sat her down on the edge of her bed to have a serious talk. The *shoulds* and *should nots*, if you will. Gracie seemed to understand that social media was a bad gig and that putting photos of herself on the internet was dangerous. She nodded at every topic I had researched to talk about, and she shook my hand, promising she wouldn't message any strangers.

She knows better.

It started as a good thing, with Gracie minding news happening around the world, showing me images of places I'd never go, and giving us something to talk about at the dinner table. After the excitement of the new toy dimmed, dinners together became less and less frequent until they were nonexistent. Gracie started wearing only black clothing, hiking her shirts up to show most of her rib cage, and responding to the *blips* and *beeps* of virtual messaging rather than chatting with me. When we did cross paths every few days or so, the phone's glow would continue to illuminate her face, accompanied by the dispassion for reality.

I started to worry about my daughter for the first time in my life.

"Hey there," I prompted three nights before our annual trip. I tapped softly on Gracie's bedroom door. It was the first time in months I'd noticed even a gap in the entrance. I didn't hear a reply but cracked open the door anyway.

"Gracie?" I poked my head in.

My daughter lay on her back in her unmade bed. She held her phone just above her face, her nose almost pressing against its screen while her fingers hotly typed a message. Mounds of black jeans and tees were lumped on the carpet throughout the surrounding cave, and stacks of *Seventeen* magazines occupied most of the space on her vanity, second in number only to a vast assortment of lipsticks and powders. The entire space smelled like hair spray.

"Dad!" she screamed, dropping the phone on her face. I couldn't help but chuckle. She grabbed the bridge of her nose immediately and moaned.

"Ugh, that's not funny!" she murmured nasally.

"Oh, I'm sorry, I didn't know I wasn't allowed to visit with my daughter," I retorted. "And it *was* funny."

Gracie was immensely thin while laying down. Her legs were slim and knobby like that of a fawn, and the skin of her arms were a light cloak to the bones underneath. If she sucked in a full breath, I guessed I could've counted at least seven of her twelve rib bones.

Maybe this is part of the growing process? I haven't noticed how thin she is . . .

"You hungry, girl? I could order pizza or subs or whatever you'd like."

I received a bitter face in response.

"Nah, I'm not hungry. Thanks though," she said nonchalantly, picking her phone up and continuing to scroll.

"Oh," I commented with disappointment. "I was hoping we might get some food and watch a movie together." I wanted to see Gracie eat something, anything. She side-eyed me at the suggestion, her thumb halted on the screen.

"I'm happy to watch a movie, but again, I'm just not hungry," she affirmed.

"Okay, did you eat lunch at least?"

"You worry too much. I did eat lunch. Go put on a movie, Dad."

Kinda bossy these days, huh?

Gracie's attitude had progressively become more intense over the last year, making me wonder if she had been introduced to her monthly cycles yet.

"Okay, what would you like to see?" I asked. I made a bet with myself that it'd be something Nicholas Sparks.

"IDK, man, just go pick something, please," she replied with an annoyed tone.

What does IDK even mean?

I obliged to her demand, though not before scouring the bathroom for evidence to some of the questions I wanted to ask her. I did happen to find a box of Playtex tampons and wondered if she was Googling how to learn to handle this sort of thing. It made me flash back to the Army days, when I was learning how to shoot guns and safely hold grenades. At least I had someone to teach me how to effectively stop bleeding for good.

I wandered to the living room and plopped down on the leather sofa. My usual spot had a dip in it that slumped inward. It was where I always sat to think when I didn't feel like going to Marmo's.

I hunched over and rested my elbows on my knees, too preoccupied with questioning my parenting skills to relax and flip through DIRECTV. I lit a Camel that was stuck in my flannel pocket just for these sorts of times.

Am I a bad father?

The question pummeled me until the smoke no longer stung my eyes awake. I drifted in and out of existence, and then fully into sand land.

The next morning, I awoke with a pillow behind my head and a blanket tucked around me. Despite Gracie's urge to be fervently disconnected, I knew she'd always be my little girl who chased around Jacky Jack. I decided right then I needed to have a talk with Gracie on this year's fishing trip, but not the sort of talk most parents were having at this age. No, I needed to chat about something a bit less complicated, but just as difficult.

One night passed by, and then another, and then as quickly as it'd leave us, our trip's day of departure had arrived. I shoved the fishing gear and coolers and sleeping bags into Red, who had aged with more rust, and scurried around the kitchen to gather the final pieces to our trip.

"Almost ready, honey?" I yelled to Gracie, who was unsurprisingly in her room.

"Yeah, be right there!"

Gracie appeared in her doorway lugging a suitcase with zippers that would detonate clothing if they were tugged open. She wore dark makeup and acid-washed shorts that made her legs skyscrapers. The tube top on her upper half must've been pasted on.

"Um, you do remember we're going to the middle of West Virginia, right?" I asked. I hoped I sounded just as confused as I was. Gracie tried lugging her bag, broken wheel and all, across the kitchen floor.

"Ugh, Dad, do we have to have this talk? Really?" she replied.

My cane fell to the ground when I stumbled over to help Gracie with her bag. "I just don't understand why you think you need all of this . . . this getup," I commented, out of breath even before reaching her.

"Does it matter?" she asked, annoyed. I think her eye roll produced enough strength for her bony arms to nudge her luggage to Red on their own.

Silence gnawed on our ears all the way to the Elk, save for the *blips* and *beeps*.

Upon arriving at our spot, Gracie stormed off to presumably grab firewood. I devised a plan to bring up my concern over Gracie's weight. If I had anything to question, it'd have to first begin with finding the root of the problem, which undoubtedly stemmed from the device chained to her wrist.

I was just finishing some organization for our sleeping arrangements when Gracie's pale stomach reflected the August sunshine from afar. She emerged from the woods with a few scrawny twigs.

"Hey, baby girl," I hollered. Gracie waved, already appearing more relaxed.

See, maybe she just needed some outdoor therapy.

Gracie moseyed to Red and opened the front passenger's side door. She rummaged for quite some time before plucking a jar of peanut butter and some Ritz from a grocery bag.

Ah perfect, she's hungry! That's a great sign.

I noted that Gracie's phone was actually in her pocket for once. Perhaps she didn't have service in this part of the world.

"Doesn't it feel good to be cut off from society for a bit?" I asked her from afar, leaning on my cane.

"Um, no, not really." She frowned. "It actually kinda stresses me out."

"Oh? And why's that?" I asked as she shoved a whole cracker in her mouth.

Between crumbs spewing and smacking peanut butter, she shook her head. "Nah, Dad, you wouldn't understand. All you understand is fishing," she said, furrowing her eyebrows and laughing playfully.

Well what the hell was that s'posed to mean?

She shoved another cracker in her mouth, leaned into Red to pull out a camp chair from the back seat, and dragged it to the Elk. I joined with my own chair and two fishing poles soon after. I brushed off the earlier, hurtful comment before casting my shot at being funny myself.

"Come here often?" I joked while unfolding my seat next to her. I dropped the fishing poles and my cane on the ground next to Gracie, who was scowling. The ping of her fishing comment loomed over me a bit more now.

"'Member when you used to eat worms and play with your imaginary friend for hours on end in this very same spot?" I reminisced.

Even the daisies still popped up after all these years. Gracie was plucking at one in her lap as I stood above her. Though disfigured, it reminded me of the limp one she offered me years ago.

"I don't ever remember eating a worm," Gracie denied. "That's disgusting."

I laughed. "They were one of your favorite things. I'm surprised you don't remember."

Gracie flashed a horrified look down at her daisy, then to the fishing poles, and then back to me. "Yeah, maybe I do remember a little. I try not to. That's gross." She cringed. "I remember Jack the most. He was a good friend." Her lips transitioned to a smile.

My heart warmed at the thought of Gracie recalling a piece of her childhood that most people often let become overgrown by adulthood.

"Are you planning on fishing here, or . . . ?" Gracie interrupted my sentimental remembering.

I shook my head back to reality. "Ah, well, I was hopin' to chat with you about a few things first, is that good with you?" I plopped down in my seat, my hands trembling a bit with nervousness.

"Uh, sure? What?" Gracie asked.

I leaned forward and plucked a daisy of my own, twirling it in between my thumb and pointer finger. I contemplated how I was going to begin a conversation with my teenage daughter about starving herself, of all things. The daisy's stem juices started crying on my fingers. I let it fall to the earth and grabbed a fishing pole.

"Have I ever told you my story about the mayfly?"

Gracie contemplated, and then shook her head. I inspected the pole.

"You see, when I was seventeen, Pa tried to talk me out of joining the Army." I adjusted the pole's line. "He and I argued about it to the point that we didn't speak with each other for months at times. It pissed me off that he wanted to control my life, but thinking back now, he was just tryin' to protect me."

Now look at me. I have half a memory.

Gracie studied me with unmoving eyes.

I continued, "One day, Pa caught me off guard and told me about the mayfly. You know, what I fly fish with. He tried to teach me this lesson about how life is short and all, and how I should do what makes me happy while I'm alive, even though he hated the thought of me joining the Army. It was the best example he could come up with to relate to me. I don't know if you've heard this, but the mayfly only lives for twenty-four hours after it emerges from the water."

Gracie shook her head and gazed toward the Elk, where thousands, if not millions, of mayflies would hatch over the course of our trip.

"Well yeah, so, the mayfly only lives for twenty-four hours at that point. When Pa told me that, it kinda gave me this epiphany and brought about an ass-ton of questions I had, like, why? Why do they only live for twenty-four hours? And, if I only had that much time left, what would I be doing? It was a nagging thought for a long time, and I joined the Army months later, because it felt like my calling at the time. If I only had one day left, I wanted to live it by fighting to protect the ones I loved."

Gracie remained silent, soaking in one of the longest conversations I'd ever had with her.

"Anyway, Gracie. If you were a mayfly, I hope you'd think about all of the things you'd want to do for each second you'd live, and I hope you'd accomplish everything in the world you'd want to do. When you stop and think about it, being the skinniest girl in school is minuscule in the grand scheme of things."

I placed my hand on Gracie's back while tears rolled down her cheeks. She was pinching what rolls of her stomach she had left. She put her head on my shoulder and sobbed for many minutes before speaking.

"But, Dad, I want to be thin like all of the girls online," she cried. "I want to *be* them. I want to wear their clothes and have boyfriends like theirs and have all the friends that they have."

Salty tears emerged from my eye wells, too.

"Honey, I can't understand how you're feeling, but I do know that being skinny doesn't automatically make you beautiful." I lifted my left arm up and relaxed it around her shoulders. "You're already amazing in the ways only *you* can be."

Gracie faced me with curtains of mascara draped on her cheeks but didn't reply. She leaned over the camp chair's arm and hugged my waist. I rubbed away a stray teardrop lingering on one eye's lashes.

"You don't have to be sorry for who you are, and you don't have to change for people to like you. Just go on loving yourself and your life. Don't do it for me. Do it for you."

Gracie nodded and released me from her embrace. She stood up, reached into her pocket, and chucked her phone as far as she could into the Elk.

13

INHABITING
FRACTURED GLASS,

—

The worst thing about being a father of a fourteen-year-old is having to witness your child live through fourteen.

We parents quake at the thought of our children being freshmen, but the children themselves metamorphose like caterpillars in their chrysalises. Boys that wandered the halls just a year before ripen into young men, the women become more mature, and every body is growing and sweating and smelling in ways they hadn't before.

While most parents were hovering over their liquor cabinets in fear of having to smack their child's hands with the Bible, I was driving Gracie to therapists and nutritionists so she could overcome her anorexia.

The first few therapist experiences were a bit kooky. I'd sit in each of their pristine, white-walled waiting rooms reading an *Esquire* or that week's sudoku until Gracie would burst out of the door in outrage, screaming that she hated me for "taking her to these assholes." I never got upset. I'd just tiptoe to her, hand her the keys to Red, and let her practice driving us home.

Not one person was striking the right chord for Gracie after several weeks of this déjà vu. Until I had an unusually long chat with Ms. Mia over at CVS during one of my Sunday med pickups in late September. Coincidentally, that woman was one helluva good unlicensed therapist according to her certified friends, and though we couldn't legally pay her for her services, she offered to speak with Gracie for free once a week at Marmo's after work. And she did.

Ms. Mia and Gracie became somewhat friends. They'd sit in the front bay window and talk of nutrition and exercise, of mean girls and attractive boys, and of all the dreams Gracie had for when she "grew up." Most of the time I only snagged murmurs of the conversations since I was usually in the back room firing and blowing glass. Other times whole conversations would fill my ears.

"Oh, and this Miles boy lives next to you?" I overheard Ms. Mia ask once. "Is he sweet?"

"Oh yeah, he's cute if *that's* what you're asking!" Gracie replied reassuringly. Ms. Mia's laugh ricocheted off the ornaments dangling above.

"In that case, why haven't you gone out together? Have you considered asking him out?"

An abrupt silence followed. Gracie cleared her throat. "Nah, not yet. The rumor is that he's going to break up with Frankie soon, though."

Frankie. And Miles! I thought I didn't have to worry about these kids anymore.

I filled Marmo's with the heat of my kiln for an hour after that conversation ended.

With all of that awkwardness aside, Gracie's BMI was back to normal by the time she was toward the end of age fifteen. All three of us knew it was because of Ms. Mia's cheerleading.

"Oh, stop it, Ben, you could've done this on your own if you'd just listen to her," Ms. Mia told me one day in late July after Gracie left Marmo's to play soccer with Miles. Ms. Mia wrapped her arms around me right then for the first time, then softly kissed my cheek. I replayed that exchange again and again in my head after it happened.

A week later, Ms. Mia became Mrs. Mia. Apparently her new boyfriend, whose name I couldn't remember, got down on his knee a few months prior. She had decided to keep the whole thing a secret and refused to wear the engagement ring outside of the house. Neither Gracie or I knew about the engagement or the wedding until she came to Marmo's one evening to tell us she'd be moving out of Clarksburg the next day. I think my heart sank more then than it had the day Naomi left.

If I was torn apart by it, Gracie was absolutely furious.

"What in the actual *fuck* do you mean you're leaving? None of us even knew you were engaged!" I recalled Gracie screaming into Ms. Mia's face after being told the news.

I'd never seen a woman more frightened than Ms. Mia at that moment, and I'd surely never observed my daughter with such rage. When Ms. Mia stormed out of Marmo's that evening, Gracie took one of the glass ornaments from the ceiling and lobbed it at her car.

"That's enough, Gracie," I asserted, attempting to hush her sobs while holding her on the ground in the driveway out front. The heartbreak felt more familiar than I'd like.

"What if we move up our annual fishing trip this year?" I offered. "I'll close up shop and we can leave a week earlier than normal. How's that sound?"

It was the only way I knew how to cope, after all.

14

GLARING AT CHANGE . . .

"Let's go already, slowpoke!" Gracie yelled at me through my bedroom door. The truth was that I wasn't ready for a two-week vacation at all. In fact, I was just waking up.

Ah fuck it, man. I'm exhausted.

"Sweetie, can I sleep a bit longer?" I had the balls to ask. "Your ole man's tired."

Her scoff clanged my eardrums. "Seriously, Dad, if you don't get your ass out of bed, I'm never going to forgive you."

Well, damn, she's excited.

"Alright, well, give me an hour then."

I drooped out of my cotton sheets, wobbled to the bathroom, and gathered my toothbrush and paste for the trip. I located my lucky green fishing cap and flung a couple flannels and Levi's over my shoulder, along with a thick jacket in the event that it'd rain. I recalled the year that Gracie and I met Gabriella at Pete's Diner and decided to pack one nice button-down shirt—just in case.

I staggered out of my room with my loot and shoved everything in the back seat. The fishing gear, camp chairs, toolbox, and all of that junk always sat together in the garage, but the car was jam-packed already. Gracie had taken it upon herself to load Rusty Red. We joked about the car's new nick-name often.

"I think we'll be ready to go soon!" I yelled to Gracie's open bedroom window. "Grab some snacks and let's hit the road!"

Gracie immediately slammed her bedroom window and raced to the car minutes later with a plastic bag full of snacks swinging in the crook of her arm. Her flowing hair, now matching the russet color of mine, was tied back in a bun. Her jeans were ripped, revealing her knees, and her white Converse were scuffed with dirt. The look reminded me of her mother.

"I got all the snacks! Let's go!" she called out, flinging the bag into the back and hopping into the driver's seat. She twisted Red's key, and it spat at us like gunfire but reluctantly hummed with the August breeze.

The sun kissed our arms, and we trekked to the Elk with the windows cranked open. There was this surreal, childlike feeling of escaping town early—as if we were rebels for taking advantage of our father-daughter trip as adults. Neither of us could stop smiling.

We pulled into the familiar gravel drive to find a sage Jeep in our usual parking spot. Its top cover was removed, revealing the vehicle's dark leather seats. A small, metal motorboat was hitched to the back and stuffed with three large coolers. The owner was nowhere in sight.

I suppose that's what we get for doing things a bit differently this year.

"Huh, I've never had this happen before. What do you think? Should we stay in our spot or go park somewhere else?" I asked, stroking my mostly gray beard and tossing Gracie a raised eyebrow.

"Find somewhere else?" Gracie asked. "This is our spot. Who cares if we make a new friend?"

I've never been good at making new friends.

I nodded convincingly. Gracie inched Red toward a parking spot that was not our own but would work all the same. Just as she shoved Red's gear into park, a shadow engulfed the sun that was striking my face and knocked on my door. It jolted my spine toward the sky.

"Pardon, I didn't mean to frighten you!" a thick voice barged through the window.

A broad-shouldered man with bristly eyebrows and hair black as ink crouched down to meet my height.

"Bonjour, I'm Eliott," he greeted, reaching a tanned hand through the window to shake my own.

This must be our Jeep guy. Was that French?

I took the man's hand firmly.

"Man, you scared me, Eliott. You came out of thin air," I said heartily.

"Right, you see, I was sitting on ze ground on ze other side of my boat's trailer when you pulled in, enjoying my lunch." He motioned toward his boat. "I zought I'd come give you a warm hello. Are you new here?"

"Nope, this is actually our spot." I thumbed toward Gracie. "We've been coming here for the last, like, thirteen years."

Eliott gaped with surprise.

"Well, bienvenue!" he said loudly. "I hope you don't mind my intrusion. Zis is my first time on ze Elk."

"Where were you before?" Gracie chimed in, leaning into the steering wheel to grab a better view of him. He rotated his stern face toward the river. His gaze fused with his memory.

"I was raised in France alongside a *fleuve*, a river, named Loire. My papa was a merchant fisherman. I lived zere my whole life until my father died from pneumonia. I left for

America to study biology not long after and eventually became a scientist."

Gracie clenched her teeth, realizing she brought up a sore subject for the stranger.

"I'm sorry to hear all that," she said, grabbing the door handle and opening the door to leave the vehicle.

Eliott transported back to us. "Life goes on, belle," he told my daughter.

Gracie slammed the door and stood outside Red, facing the stranger. She rested her elbows on the car roof. "My name isn't *belle*, but nice guess."

I cracked the passenger door open and Eliott bopped out of the way. I stood up and shoved my cane to the earth.

"That was French, my dear," I mentioned to Gracie from behind. I bore into the man's dark eyes before saying, "I'm Ben, and that's my daughter, Grace."

"Ah, Grace. Zat is *le répit* to some in France. A relief," Eliott said. He smiled innocently and swiped a hand through the coils of his hair, wicking away beads of sweat in the wrinkles of his forehead in the process. He cast a glance toward his boat. "Do you two want to go for a ride?"

15

THEN WE EMBARKED UNSAID WATERS.

———

"I'm really not in the mood for a boat ride. Why don't you go out and I'll set up camp," Gracie suggested while rummaging for something in the back seat.

"You sure?" I asked, watching from afar as Eliott unhitched his boat. He wore tall, rubber fishing boots with green cargo pants and a white T-shirt.

He's an odd one.

"Yeah, I'm sure. I'd rather go for a walk. A boat ride's just not my speed right now," she shrugged. "Ya get it? *Speed?* For a speedboat?" She chuckled and dramatized the pun with a smack on her knee.

"Aha, very funny," I retorted sarcastically. "Alright, well, if you're sure, I'll get out of your hair then."

I spun around and my cane and I hobbled to Eliott.

"You about ready, *ami*?" I questioned him.

Eliott moved the second of the three coolers to the back seat of his Jeep.

"Oh, you speak *français* now, huh?" he teased.

"Just took a few lessons from some mates while in the Army," I said, tapping my cane on my knee. "Hence why I have this bum leg."

"*Oui*, I was wondering about ze cane. Will ze motion of ze boat hurt you?" he asked.

"Nah, nothing I can't handle. I'll even help you drag this thing into the water."

I slung my cane into the boat and lifted its back end up while Eliott hoisted the front. We collectively shuffled downhill through the tall grass to the Elk. I waved to Gracie on the shore after I boosted myself onboard and scooted to the front.

"See ya soon, doll! Don't get eaten by a bear!"

Gracie melted into the woods.

"That's never funny, Dad! But I love you anyway!" The trees echoed her *I love you* back to me over and over.

Eliott had us rest on the calm water just offshore before roaring the engine. Dragonflies the color of blood swirled around us, as did the beloved mayflies. Both species were in their mating season. One pair of copulating mayflies landed on the boat's ledge next to my hand. I jerked my hand to my lap.

"Beautiful creatures, aren't zey?" Eliott commented.

Beautiful? They're pretty ugly to me.

"Why do you say that?" I asked, raising an eyebrow and squinting down at the couple.

Eliott pointed a finger at them. "Look at zem! Look at zeir wings picking up bits of ze sun, and ze way zeir bodies curve."

I leaned in. Startled, the mayflies zoomed from the boat to the sky. For a brief moment, I saw a rainbow ricochet through their transparent wings. My eyes followed them until they became black dots on the cloud above.

"Yeah, I guess they're alright," I replied while thinking about how they'd die tomorrow. "Did ya know that these guys only live for twenty-four hours in this stage? If that?"

I thought about the time I told Gracie that, and she chucked her cell phone in the water.

"Ah, *mon ami*, I *did* know zat."

"Really?" My eyebrows raised. "For some reason I didn't think that was widespread knowledge."

Eliott grinned and lowered his head. I noticed he was rubbing his feet together, chafing the rubber toes of his boots enough so they'd squeak.

"I actually specialize in ze study of the mayfly. I know a lot about zem," he said.

"Oh? What do you mean, 'specialize'?"

Eliott was quiet for some time. "I just play with zeir genetics is all." He stopped the squeaking. "Ready to see ze Elk?"

I nodded, and Eliott pulled the cord to the boat's engine. We darted swiftly upstream into the open water.

Just minutes of going fifteen miles per hour on the Elk took me to spots upstream that I'd never been with Gracie over the years. As Eliott sped me to unfamiliar portions of the West Virginian river, I noted the pine trees were taller, the forest was thicker, and the rocks in the water jutted higher. The current was stronger, too, making the boat's engine whine with the increased horsepower.

"Do ya think there's a waterfall coming down from upstream? Is that why the current's stronger here?" I yelled despite the wind drowning my voice.

Eliott slowed the throttle and we sputtered to a stop, letting the Elk drag us downstream.

"Yeah, I'm sure zere is. We'll have to come explore zat with your daughter tomorrow," he mentioned.

I cleared my throat. "You better not try anything on her. I'm going to say that just this once."

Eliott belched out a laugh that led him to grab his stomach, lean back, and fall from his seat. His rubber boots kicked in the air. It took him a minute to gain composure, though I wasn't amused.

"Sir, I would never. I'm many, many moons older zan her," he chuckled, pushing himself back onto his seat. "I promise you zat ship has sailed for me, in more ways zan you know . . ."

And no ships will ever sail there.

Eliott became a bit somber after his last comment. I didn't ask why, but I did enjoy the serenity around us instead. The trees were already starting to take on autumn hues—reds and oranges dotted the valley—and a trout burst out of the water just a few feet away from us. I stared in awe at the life around us and wondered for a moment if I was dreaming.

"Want to hear what I do with ze mayflies?" Eliott asked, interrupting the serenity.

I tasted sweat on my upper lip.

"Sure, I'd love to," I muttered, wiping my forehead. "What about this? Let's get back to camp, I'll fish us a late lunch, and you can tell Gracie and I at the same time."

Eliott nodded. Sweat lathered above his dark brows. "Deal, *l'homme.*"

I fixed my eyes on the tail of a sizable fish swaying by the boat's side just before Eliott cranked the engine cord. The boat roared, and the fish bolted to the depths of the Elk.

On the trip back to our spot, the wind tousled my hair and filled my cheeks. Life zoomed on either side of me, and everything straight ahead seemed so clear. I recognized the tree line, the reservoir, and the opening to the gravel drive. My eyes darted to Red, the forest, the bank in search of Gracie. I almost didn't spot her right in front of us, emerging through the water's surface, her hand on her nose and her hair sopping over her face. I didn't even know she liked to swim.

I hurled myself backward and reached for the rudder, thrusting it as far right as I could to avoid hitting Gracie. The immediate change in direction snagged the Elk's waters and, for a fleeting millisecond, catapulted the boat in the air before it capsized.

I heard Gracie's screams, and I thought still her echoing *I love you's,* as my head crunched against a submerged rock.

16

WE DANCED
BENEATH STARS,

———

Here's the thing about life—the entire time you're in it, you wish it felt like that one moment you danced in the desert, celebrated your fifth birthday playing tag with all of your friends from kindergarten, or watched snow fall on the limbs of towering pine trees while crunching through heaps of winter with your dad. The fact of the matter is most of our days feel like that one when your sister tied a string to your tooth and slammed the door, when your cat went missing, or when your aunt got so drunk on New Year's Eve she puked in your hair. It's a sad truth, really. But somehow, falling to the sand beneath a desert sky, palms facing the Milky Way, makes the bleeding gums and soiled hair worth enduring.

In the Army, I often thought about my twilight zone—that moment between life and death where most tend to flash through their memories. I wondered if perhaps the webs of time were nonexistent in this space so we had the opportunity to experience everything all over again on standby—so we could shake our heads at the times we thought we could be more human and laugh at the moments when we were nothing but. When the bomb exploded and took most of my memory, you can imagine I was geared up to go through some of this ghost-of-Christmas-past shit.

When I woke up that day, I didn't even know I had been revived. Maybe the Almighty wasn't ready for me then. This time, though, was unlike before, and not the expanded slice of orange dusk I had imagined when I had air in my lungs.

Still, it was all the time I needed to slip into my reel and cast one last memory into the sky:

Gracie was squatting on the shore of the Elk. Her tutu swayed in the slight breeze of that August day just before her seventh birthday.

"There it is, Daddy!" she screamed at, I assumed, her reflection. I was onshore sitting in my favorite blue camp chair, taking a drag from a cigarette. Life was simple then for Gracie and me. We hadn't had to deal with her mom's leaving, bullies like Frankie, or anorexia.

The tall, black rain boots Gracie wore swallowed her slim legs but were just short enough that I could spot the mud crusted on her knees. Mayflies darted around her in the overgrown grass as she picked a daisy and held it to her nose. Innocence emanated from the gesture.

Gracie careened toward me, giggling, with the daisy in hand. Two of the petals had flown off in the wind by the time she reached me. She held it up and the daisy flopped over her hand.

"This is yours," she said to me.

It was such a fragile, little thing. Just like life then. I stuck the flower in the cupholder next to my Camels. She twirled away, her blonde hair whipping behind her as she ran to play in her world. Things seemed to get dimmer then as she ran, and she ran, and she ran with her imaginary friend, Jack.

I called to her from such a distance, afraid to lose her light. I could still see her petting cattails and muttering to Jack.

"What are you and Jack talking about?" I yelled, my voice echoing in what didn't look like the Elk at all. My eyes scanned the area. It was nighttime now—not how I remembered this conversation.

Gracie hesitated.

"Hurry, Gracie, I don't think I have much time!" I yelled again, my words echoing into the darkness.

"I want to meet an astronaut, Daddy. I want him to take me to space so I can touch a star! The world will be beautiful from up above, with the stars!"

I could almost feel them now. An elevation crept within me.

"And what about Jack? Does he want to go too?" I inquired, reaching toward my daughter, hoping she'd run back to me.

Gracie remained quiet and then said reluctantly, "He has to stay with you, Daddy. And you have to go to space."

I sobbed. "I'm no astronaut, Gracie. I can't give you the stars." I wrapped my hands around my body, pretending I was hugging her from afar.

"That's okay, Daddy. Then you'll become something better." She blew me a kiss and hugged herself, too.

Things were fading past twilight in the depths of the Elk, and I was no longer a part of that same world where it was hard enough to breathe. No, in this place, I could finally exhale easily. That meant, wherever I was, I could become the desert sky Gracie dances beneath.

And I'm convinced, at least in my final gasp, that becoming the sky for someone is just as good as giving a star.

17

WE REELED IN THE ELK,

————

I swallowed another mouthful of water, screaming for my dad beneath the surface, screeching desperately as bubbles cascaded from my mouth.

"Daaaoowwd!" I managed to cry one last time before emerging from the Elk again. I treaded water temporarily as Eliott frantically sloshed around in the river near his overturned boat. My hope dimmed, but I surged back into the darkness below, kicking my feet every which way and stretching my hands out as far as they would extend—reaching for a burgundy shirt sleeve, maybe, or a pack of cigarettes. Anything.

Please don't let this be the end.

I burst through the surface again, gulping air, flopping the hair out of my eyes. Eliott was now on land in a fetal position.

Oh God, please, please don't let this happen.

I shuddered uncontrollably while trying to stay afloat.

Don't give up on me, Eliott.

A throaty bellow escaped from my windpipe and struck the trees. Eliott's eyes rose to me, swollen with remorse. He shook his head into the earth and waved at me to come ashore.

A baseball lodged in my throat when I yearned to yell, "No, he's still alive! Why the *fuck* are you not still searching?"

Not enough time for that.

I didn't waste my breath. Instead, I dove back under with as much energy as my legs could muster. My veins raged with the thought that my dad would be nothing other than a drowned fisherman to many. He was the only person to ever love me. Period.

But a bloody, drowned fisherman is what the papers will say.

If I ever questioned the possibility to cry underwater, I defied it right then.

Hours later, I continued to flush in and out of the Elk while the sun closed in on the horizon. Eliott had left with his Jeep to try and find help, or at the very least, locate phone service to make a few calls. He told me I shouldn't be there for them.

This can't be real.

Down I went, again.

This just can't be real. It can't be.

I couldn't distinguish between water and tears any longer.

Why would Dad've done that? I wasn't even close to him . . . I heard them coming. I felt the water. I knew they were there. I mean, Jesus Christ, does he think I'm stupid? I know when a speedboat is coming.

My stomach was cement, and my heart was a jackhammer. I thought with the heaviness that maybe I'd be resting on the bottom of our August sanctuary soon, too.

God, I'm so sorry, Dad. This is my fault.

Anger swam alongside me, hounded by looming guilt.

I mean, fuck, you know I don't even like to swim.

18

WE PUDDLED THE WATERCOLORS.

———

"Hey, Eliott, thanks for coming," I uttered robotically, just like I greeted Ms. Mia and the few others.

I was standing on the steps of the brick-lined entrance to the funeral home where my dad's wake was being held. The soft tissue below my eyes revealed my exhaustion, and the black jeans and band tee I wore were the same ones I lived in when I got the call that my father had been found.

It had been a week since that night when I slept on the kitchen floor at home, yet I couldn't disrobe from the familiar scent of the Elk, of the forest, of August. It was the guilt, or so my therapist told me in his fucking annoyingly calm voice. I wish I could feel as pleasant as he sounded.

"How are you holding up, *ma chérie*?" Eliott must've asked several times. His eyes were also hefty, like a pouch of sugar had been stuffed below them.

"The same, really," I admitted.

Eliott knew how guilty I felt with everything going on and part of me loathed him for being there that day. Even if I became consumed with hate, he was indisputably a nice guy. He held my head in his lap while I sobbed in the passenger seat of Red for several hours the night of the accident, and followed closely behind Red when I located the energy to drive back to Clarksburg the next day.

The accident.

Every now and then, the thought tormented me. In my head, the corny joke I made just before Dad climbed into the boat repeated over and over again. The pun reverberated in my temples in front of Eliott, and I straightened my spine a bit for composure.

"Ah, I understand. I'm next to you," he placated, his hand on my shoulder. He leaned in for a hug and I attempted sucking his strength into my pores. For a brief moment I thought I succeeded, with Eliott floating into me just like when a strip of fog gets sucked into a larger cloud. But he pulled back into his own entity.

"Pardon, I'm going to pay my respects," he dismissed himself.

I nodded and batted away the smell of death and dusty curtains when Eliott creaked open the ancient oak door to the funeral home. I eyeballed the sun striking the gray tile that lined the entrance to where my father rested.

Why is the sun even shining any longer?

I twisted to my left and threw up in a bush. I sat on the cement steps after to contain my nausea.

Twenty minutes later, the hinges of the door squealed, and I smelled the dust on Eliott's suit jacket before he had a chance to speak.

"I know you're sorry, you don't have to say it," I mumbled, my palm holding my head up.

"Yes, I did want to say zat . . ." his voice trailed. I twisted behind me to find the pensive Frenchman rubbing the toes of his loafers together.

"Yeah, and what else did you wanna say?" I asked.

He stood straight up then.

"Well, I wanted to invite you to my home where my lab is. I'm a scientist. I explained what I really do to your papa right before he, well . . . I zink you'd be interested in seeing what I've been experimenting on ze last several years," he said.

My jaw had dropped somewhere between Eliott inviting me into his home and calling Dad *papa*.

The fucking nerve.

"You think I really want to spend more time with you than I have to, aye?" I asked.

Eliott rubbed the toes of his shoes again. The cognac leather had thick, brown scuffs around the curved edges. It must've been something he did out of nervousness.

Tenderly he said, "I just zought you'd be interested in ze experiment. Zat's all, *ma chérie*."

I scowled at him and whirled away, focused on the sky and its purple-and-orange watercolor. The hues boomeranged toward the side of the earth where the sun wasn't setting.

Eliott stood behind me for several minutes before saying, "I'm going to leave you my address still, just in case you'd like to visit sometime."

Out of the corner of my eye, I saw he placed a crumpled sticky note by my side with some atrocious writing. It resembled an address, maybe.

How would I be able to read that shit even if I wanted to?

I thought I could make out *the mayfly* written at the top. Before I could confirm the hieroglyphics, I noticed brake lights flickering at the stop sign down the road, and the Jeep that was parked on the curb in front of me was gone.

19

AND THE MAYFLIES—

———

Two nights. That's how long it took until my entire imagination was engulfed by mayflies.

What did Eliott mean by experiment? *Who let him be a scientist, anyway?*

I'd scoff as I watched a mayfly zip around the kitchen as I ate my Lucky Charms. While showering, one would play in the suds near my unpainted toes. When driving Red to visit Ava, I'd happen upon one catching a nap in the afternoon sun on the dashboard.

Then they'd all die within twenty-four hours.

I mean, what the hell, Eliott.

On the third day since my father's wake, I drove almost two hours to a woodland village in search of 77 Brookland Avenue. Eliott's Jeep was a clear giveaway of his whereabouts in the less than small town deep in West Virginia. I parked Red in the dirt driveway, tromped across the grass lawn, and knocked on Eliott's cabin-like door. I imagined a freshly hatched mayfly looming over my shoulder.

It took him several minutes to answer my knock. His stumbling and shoving of chairs emanated through the door while I tried to wait patiently, passing time by examining the treetops. The sound of dead bolts liberating their sockets echoed over lifetimes.

"Ah, zere you are, mademoiselle. I knew you'd come one of zese days," Eliott said in the doorway, exasperated. He wore a white lab coat with a burgundy flannel beneath it.

That looks like Dad's flannel.

Sadness clawed at my gut.

"Yeah, I figured you'd think that," I grumbled, settling a hand on my stomach. "I'm interested in whatever the hell you're doing here, Eliott. Please show me so I can close this chapter of my life."

He frowned, perhaps partially because he could tell I had not been well. His thick eyebrows curved inward and intensified the creases on his forehead.

"The whole point of zis is zat zere wouldn't necessarily be *just* an end."

I immediately felt bad for discounting years of this man's hard work.

"Well, you know, I'm sorry, you understand what I mean."

I didn't intend for that to come out so harsh.

Eliott had turned away long before I apologized. His back was to me when he waved me inside the cabin.

"Would you like some water?" he asked when entering the kitchen straight ahead. "I make a *mean* espresso, too, mademoiselle." The kitchen was quite modern, unlike the exterior of his home. He drifted toward a half-full glass of water resting on the granite countertop and took a quick sip.

"Uh, no, I'm okay. I am tired, though. I've stayed up late the past few nights, thinking about mayflies."

He released his gulp and choked on a laugh. "Well . . . I'm glad ze intrigue consumed you in such a way!" he said loudly.

I pretended to laugh along.

"Alright, well if you would like to see what I'm working on and zen head home, I understand. Let's be on our way." He clapped his hands together and nodded in the direction of the short hallway.

I wonder if he could tell that was a fake laugh.

The wood floor expanded into a stairwell that led up to a second story of the cabin. Black-and-white images of the Eiffel Tower and a funny-looking old man with thick, round glasses lined the stairway to the upstairs.

"Zat's my papa," he pointed out in passing. "Good man, he was."

Eliott lingered at the top of the climb to stare at one photo in particular. He and a woman stood in front of a merry-go-round, French-kissing, for a lack of better words. Eliott was younger then, maybe my age.

Old girlfriend?

We hooked right toward a room with a closed, solid wood door.

"Zat was Maddie. She was my girlfriend," he acknowledged without me asking.

Uh, odd you still have that photo, you weirdo.

He continued, "She died unexpectedly in a motorcycle accident when I first started university. It was a rainy night, but she loved riding her bike more zan anything."

I'm such a dick.

"Oh, I'm so sorry," I replied with regret.

"Well, she's in part why I am who I am and why I do what I do," he countered with an optimistic tone, "and zat's why I wanted to share zis with you, too."

Eliott opened the heavy door to reveal a plastic-wrapped, kitchen-like oasis. Rows of white, unfolded tables lined the space, dotted with microscopes, several aquariums brimming with ecosystems, and the largest sink I'd ever seen. Hundreds of glass slats like the ones I'd used in biology class lined the countertops among notebooks etched with hieroglyphics that matched Eliott's handwriting.

I'm certain my eyes could've rolled out onto the floor.

"Holy hell, no kidding," I released under my breath, surprised that the scientist thing was true. "What in the world do you do in here?"

Eliott's face was smug. This was his environment, his space—this was his version of the Elk.

"I play with genetics . . . lately, I've been playing with mayfly genetics."

He scuffed the fronts of his sneakers together.

"Zat's why I was out on ze Elk zat day," he said. "I was hoping to collect more specimens for some experiments."

So . . . basically, my dad's death was part of a science experiment?

I inhaled sharply to allow my immediate anger to dissipate.

"So like . . . what kind of experiments do you do then?" My eyes danced around the room, attempting to piece things together.

Eliott gently took my arm and guided me to a tall, cracked-leather stool with wheels. He patted my shoulder and pointed at the seat, motioning for me to sit. Then he put a hand on each of my shoulders and stared into my eyes. I scrunched my neck and leaned back from the closeness.

"Grace, I do experiments to extend life for ze beings zat don't have a long life to live."

I stared through him into the distance. I was confused . . . and yet, I almost thought I understood. Almost. Because of that, I wanted to peel out of my skin.

"What the fuck do you mean?"

Eliott stepped back and swept toward one of the aquariums. "I want to show you, not tell you. Zat is why you are here in my house."

20

THEY LINGERED

—

E liott scooped up a small butterfly net that rested beside one of the tanks. He shoved back the encasement's glass lid and stuck the net inside, twisting his wrist about. I examined from afar at first, but inched closer each minute.

"Zere's something about ze way zat life is fleeting zat makes it seem so pointless yet so fascinating," he remarked, still whipping around the net. "Someone once asked me, 'Would you extend your life if you had ze power to do so?' I thought about zat for a long time before I answered ze question. And in ze end, years later, I told Maddie zat—*oop*, I caught one."

Eliott reached his hand into the ecosystem and cupped his free hand over the mouth of the net. I wandered close enough to hear the water system churning and smell the dirt from inside.

"What is it?" I asked, peering at Eliott. He pulled the net from the tank and hung it before me.

"Zis is a mayfly. But, he's just not any mayfly," he said proudly. "Zis one emerged two years ago."

"It what!" I clutched my chest and stepped back.

"You heard right. Two years," he reassured with a grin. "I told Maddie zat if I could extend my own life, I would so

I could live all of ze days she would. It wasn't long after zat when I got ze call from my papa zat she had died. Zen shortly after zat, he also went. I felt destroyed and came to ze United States knowing what I had to do."

Eliott flipped the net upside down so the mayfly would land in his hand. He removed it from all captivity and held it in front of me.

"Jesus Christ, man, how is that possible?" I asked, my heart palpating as if I'd just completed a marathon. I flashed into the cobwebs of memory and recollected my dad telling me about the mayfly only living twenty-four hours all those summers ago:

"Have I ever told you my story about the mayfly?" Dad asked me.

I thought about it for a moment, then shook my head. My dad rarely told stories . . . he taught me with actions, like when we made our own flies after mom left. So, when I motioned that I hadn't heard this tale, Dad frowned and continued inspecting his fishing pole. It took him a while to find the right words, but he did.

"You see, when I was seventeen, Pa tried to talk me out of joining the Army . . ." He adjusted the pole's line. "He and I argued about it to the point that we didn't speak with each other for months at times. It pissed me off that he wanted to control my life, but thinking back now, he was just tryin' to protect me," Dad said.

This intrigued me, hearing about this bracket of my father's life he had never shared before. It was like reading an old textbook and highlighting something that read a bit different than in all the new releases.

Dad continued, "One day, Pa caught me off guard and told me about the mayfly. You know, what I fly fish with. He tried to teach me this lesson about how life is short and all, and how I should do what makes me happy while I'm alive, even though he hated the thought of me joining the Army. It was the best example he could come up with to relate to me. I don't know if you've heard this, but the mayfly only lives for twenty-four hours after it emerges from the water."

I remembered looking out at the Elk where I'd witnessed thousands of mayflies hatch every August. Now thinking back, their tiny lives were all a twenty-four-hour time bomb.

"Well, yeah, so the mayfly only lives for twenty-four hours at that point. When Pa told me that, it kinda gave me this epiphany and brought about an ass-ton of questions I had, like, why? Why do they only live for twenty-four hours? And, if I only had that much time left, what would I be doing? It was a nagging thought for a long time, and I joined the Army months later, because it felt like my calling at the time. If I only had one day left, I wanted to live it by fighting to protect the ones I loved."

I remained silent then, soaking in all of the life lessons he was trying to thrust into the longest conversation we'd ever had.

The last thing I remember from that day besides throwing my phone in the water was this:

"Anyway, Gracie. If you were a mayfly, I hope you'd think about all of the things you'd want to do for each second you'd live, and I hope you'd accomplish everything in the world you'd want to do."

Eliott had been mumbling science gibberish in my haze for some time, and the next statement brought me back to reality.

"Overall, it took a lot of trial and error, as you can imagine. It was, more or less, easy . . . it just took an accurate and proportionate combination of coding from different insects to concoct a mayfly zat could have an extended chance at life."

"I can't believe all of this!" I exclaimed, pretending I had just listened to his earthshaking science lesson. "My dad would just love this."

I could feel the wells of my eyes beginning to fill. I focused on Eliott's palm where the bug's thin, brown body rested peacefully. It flicked its opaque wings to threaten flying away, I was certain.

"I'm glad you like him. I zought you'd take something away from knowing why I was zere ze day your dad died. I want to create more flies just like zis one, and zen someday, when I feel my purpose is fulfilled, I can sell zem to the government to evaluate zeir need."

A hammer thudded my heart into my large intestine.

"*Sell* them?" I hissed. "What do you mean, *sell them*?"

"Let me reiterate, *ma chérie*, zat when my *purpose* is fulfilled, I will have to sell zem," he said, taking a finger and gently stroking one of the mayfly's wings. "Imagine if I just started sending zem off into ze world. Even just zis one. Zat could have a monumental impact on ze environment as we know it. Swarms of mayflies could hover for years. It could even be like a plague."

A rumble of giggles leaked out of my throat, and I released a roar of bellyaching laughter in this lab. In the middle of West Virginia. In the light of my father's death. Eliott's face contorted into confusion, wondering why I had transformed into a hyena. He had not foreshadowed things correctly.

I lunged forward and snatched the mayfly with one hand, pivoting toward the door. After shoving open and racing through the lab entrance, I brought my hands together mid-stride and made a home for the bug in between my hands.

Eliott trailed behind me, screaming, though he was much slower than me. My legs flew down the stairs, my hair whipping past Eliott's dad and Maddie, and I sprinted down the hallway, through the modern kitchen, and jiggled open the front door. My lungs seethed as I ran up to Red and lifted my eyes toward the treetops.

Eliott finally appeared at his door, heaving.

"You have no idea what impact you'll have if you do zat!" he bellowed from afar.

I thought of my father and the brief time he had lived. I thought of the moments, especially the Augusts, we would never have together. I knew then, with life fluttering in my cupped hands, that if I had the choice to extend life I always would.

I laughed up at the sun as I opened my hands and cast the mayfly to the sky.

21

IN OUR ENDLESS AUGUSTS.

———

The mayfly's wings sputtered as it whipped into the air, and when it caught wind, it zoomed upward. I squinted from the sun, my arms still in the air, and traced the minuscule fly's pathway as it became a dark star in the daylight.

"Go bring a longer life to others!" My voice rang while my vision faded into the treetops, remembering how I always wanted to touch a star:

I admired my reflection in the Elk while my dad smoked a cigarette in his blue camp chair, like always. I wore my favorite thing in the world—a pink tutu and rain boots—and had twirled with dragonflies alongside the river with Jack most of the day. Clay crusted over my knees and those goddamn bangs kept getting caught on my eyelashes.

A daisy poked out of the thick muck by the Elk. It was the only one I saw that day among the wildflowers, and I knew I had to pick it. I bent closer to the water, snapped the stem from the ground, and galloped to where Dad sat. I felt mortified when I held it up to him and the thing limped over.

He just smiled and thanked me, coughing in the process. Relieved that he reacted positively, I whipped around and ran back to where I left my imaginary friend by the Elk. Shortly after, Dad called me over.

"What are you and Jack talking about tonight?" he asked me, nodding to Jack. I told him it was a secret, but I didn't think Jack would mind if I shared.

I whispered, "We're talking about the stars, Dad, and how wonderful it would be to fly into space and touch one. I promised Jack that one day we'd meet an astronaut and that the astronaut would let me touch a star and maybe even bring one home! Wouldn't that be great? I think it'd be so cool to see how beautiful the world is from up above the stars."

I waited to see what Dad would say, but all he said was, "Oh, I see, well that's nice, sweetie. You and Jack go play a little longer."

I hoped he'd tell me he would become an astronaut so I could make this wish come true, but he didn't. So instead, I pretended to laugh, took Jack's hand, and skipped back to the river.

I rejoined the towering August trees and the sky, where I had just released something that could have a butterfly effect of change on the world. I lowered my head and stared at Red. In its rust, I thought about how, all this time, my imaginary friend Jack was a rendition of my father who I could easily play games with and talk to without having to fish. It was silly thinking of it now, because I learned an endless amount about patience, self-acceptance, love, and loss in each August day I spent on the Elk. A vision emerged:

Dad told me to step aside while he prepped his stance for a cast. One foot set back on the Elk's bank and the other rippled the water. He made sure I was far enough back, set the line, and gently grabbed the cork grip on his pole. Everything aligned just so. Jack and I awed at how the rod gained tension and arced behind Dad, as if gaining enough momentum to whip the setting sun. Then he paused, as did everything around him. Somehow, in this frozen piece of time, Dad managed to glance at me to see if I was watching. Golden sunlight silhouetted his form and a smile dashed his face as he loitered in his favorite moment.

Pausing. Is. Essential.

Right then, before attempting to escape Eliott's wrath or open the door to Red, I paused. And I felt in that narrow instant, with my hand on the car door and the limitless mayfly buzzing somewhere above, my dad had become something better than an astronaut.

He was the sky that would envelop my every day, and that was just as good as receiving a star.

Traveling to space
Seemed like a good idea
When we were young.
The fragments of us
Scabbed over with yellow paint
When we crescendoed
Into little, smokeless fires.
Denial disrobes me still—
The tapestry undone and exposed;
I let our snags untangle
To vow a new thread.
You had a skinny love then,
Inhabiting fractured glass,
Glaring at change . . .
Then we embarked unsaid waters.
We danced beneath stars,
We reeled in the Elk,
We puddled the watercolors.
And the mayflies—
They lingered
In our endless Augusts.

ABOUT THE AUTHOR

Taylor Kickbush is a user experience engineer and first-time author. She's not a fly fisherwoman or a parent but has a deep admiration for the outdoors and the different scopes of the world. Taylor has been a digital marketing intern in London, England, a project management intern in Washington, DC, a journalist in Western New York, and a blogger of the World Wide Web. "The District" is now what she calls home, though she apparently does her best writing while traveling—most notably in France, Mexico, and Peru. Among the places she has seen and traveled, the imagination has by far been the most fascinating.

ACKNOWLEDGMENTS

———

Emphasizing how many lunches I skipped, social hours I missed, or nights I forwent sleep so I could remain hunched over my keyboard does not shed light on the people in my life that made *Endless in August* possible. Without the support and encouragement from those listed below, Ben and Gracie would have remained unshared characters. Because of them their story exists. Thank you:

Michael Bailey and **Emily Price**, who you'd refer to as editors, but I know as miracle workers.

Tara Capece, who first helped me wade through my "I'm a terrible writer!" phase and told me to take a deep breath and keep writing.

Thao Nhi Dang, **Nocole Gonzalez**, and **Margaret Haile-mariam**, who entered my life and made me feel valuable at a time when I needed it most.

Dan and **Beverly Gabel**, my maternal grandparents, who helped teach me how to read.

Bill and **Kyllan Gilmore**, who inspired me with their unpublished writings of "The Borgon Frog" and, with their philosophical stories, helped me formulate the fabric of an insect living longer than it should.

Linda Gilmore, a valuable (and ruthless) editor who has the power to influence any soul to admire all things wild.

Alayna Kehr, the illustrator of *Endless in August*'s cover and the forever sister I never had.

The Kehr Family, who became a family I cherished long before our bloodlines were connected.

Eric Koester, who convinced me to take part in the Creator Institute and become an author because, "There's never a good time to write a book. You just have to start."

Susan and **Todd Kickbush**, my mom and dad, who gave me the nickname "Grace" and the world.

Martha Kickbush, my paternal grandmother, who encouraged me to travel everywhere and anywhere.

Maureen Milliken, a stranger who lived in a dorm room down the hall from me at St. Bonaventure University and became a forever best friend overnight.

Alexia Nal, a friendship made in London that transitioned to Washington, DC, proven to withstand thousands of coffee dates, vent sessions, and afternoon walks.

New Degree Press, my publisher that helped this journey travel into your heart and hands.

Patrick Vecchio, who taught me the importance of three things: humor, avoiding clichés, and Bob Marley.

Denny Wilkins, a dear professor of journalism at St. Bonaventure University who lectured me less on how to write and more about how to tell the story that deserved to be told.

* * *

Thank you also to the individuals below, who preordered my book in its initial stages and helped me reach my first-time author goals:

Joseph Anello	Ricardo Figueroa
Caryn and Mark Benton	Lori Gabel
Alexandria Broyles	Emelyn Gilmore
Julie Burek	Kyllan Gilmore
Tara Capece	Tiegan Gilmore
Eric Cheng	William and Linda Gilmore
Rosanne M. Chesbro	Margaret Hailemariam
Taylor Christie	Kimberly Haller
John Cochrane	Veronica Hamilton
Casaundra Cramer	Brittany Hirschman
Becca Crosson	Paige Hollenbeck
Janelle Curtis	William Holzerland
Thao Nhi Dang	Alayna Kehr
Taylor Dechow	Rebecca Kehr
Barbara Dempsey	Stephanie Kennedy
Jacob Everhart	Spencer Kerr

Rajiv Khanna
Martha Kickbush
Susan and Todd Kickbush
Eric Koester
Rebecca Laughlin
Bryan Lawson
Anne Lee
Amanda Lippincott
Mearl and Michelle Lulas
Katie Macakanja
Christopher Man
Flor Mandujano
Terry Mansfield
Caleb McGuire
Mark Mellinger
Sarah Miller
Maureen Milliken
Paige A. Mosher
Lucas Myzel
Alexia Nal
Charlotte Nal
Nichella Nal
Meghan Nelson
Michaela Nolan
Teresa L. Oger
Brittney Olszewski

Courtney Pendino
Kim Perkins
Sean Pine
Jacob Pound
Katie Povhe
Carol Flanagan Propp
Daniel Pulaski
Gerrie Reid
Nancy Riesbeck
Cody D. Rutherford
Lloyd Scharf
Georgia Shaw
Katie Stang
Shannon Styles
Mikaela Thelen
Kathy Thompson
Kyle Trietley
Saleheh Vahaji
Jon-Erik Valetti
Samantha Van Wicklin
Will Walters
Brianna Weinaug
Hayley Wilkins
Christopher Wodeshick
Mohammed Zaatari

Made in the USA
Middletown, DE
13 August 2020

15302739R00080